Whose dark or troubled mind will you step into next? Detective or assassin, victim or accomplice? How can you tell reality from delusion when you're spinning in the whirl of a thriller, or trapped in the grip of an unsolvable mystery? When you can't trust your senses, or anyone you meet; that's when you know you're in the hands of the undisputed masters of crime fiction.

Writers of the greatest thrillers and mysteries on earth, who inspired those that followed. Their books are found on shelves all across their home countries – from Asia to Europe, and everywhere in between. Timeless tales that have been devoured, adored and handed down through the decades. Iconic books that have inspired films, and demand to be read and read again. And now we've introduced Pushkin Vertigo Originals – the greatest contemporary crime writing from across the globe, by some of today's best authors.

So step inside a dizzying world of criminal masterminds with **Pushkin Vertigo**. The only trouble you might have is leaving them behind.

AUGUSTO DE ANGELIS

THE MYSTERY OF THE THREE ORCHIDS

Pushkin Vertigo
71–75 Shelton Street
London, WC2H 9JQ

First published in Italian as
Il mistero delle tre orchidee by Aurora in 1942

First published by Pushkin Vertigo in 2016

1 3 5 7 9 8 6 4 2

ISBN 978 1 782271 72 7

Text designed and typeset by Tetragon, London

Printed and bound by CPI Group (UK) Ltd, Croydon CR0 4YY

CRISTIANA O'BRIAN REQUESTS
THE HONOUR OF YOUR COMPANY AT
THE PRESENTATION OF HER NEW SPRING COLLECTION
ON 9 MARCH FROM 15.30 ONWARDS.
BY INVITATION ONLY.

A blue envelope, long and rectangular. A blue card. In the top left corner, a white dove pierced by a long, sharp golden pin: the logo of Cristiana O'Brian: Dresses, Capes, Furs, Corso del Littorio 14.

Fifty of these small cards had been sent out, all of them strictly personal. But fifty-two of them arrived, and even the two that both Signora O'Brian and Marta, who prided herself on knowing everything that happened in the fashion house on Corso del Littorio, knew nothing about bore the words: By invitation only.

Who would have imagined that a dead body lay in the "museum of horrors" at the O'Brian Fashion House? Between the wooden-and-horsehair mannequins and, like them, immobile. Yet on its face, a terrifying sneer. The only one of them to have a head and a face...

If the Kansas City Penitentiary hadn't ruled that prisoners doing forced labour in the coal mines could obtain a reduced penalty for extra productivity, the body would not have ended up on Cristiana O'Brian's bed.

And a glass necklace would have remained just that—instead of serving a purpose as tragic as it was final.

DAY ONE: THURSDAY

1

Her throat was tightening. She wanted to scream. One scream, just one, would free her of this awful feeling of suffocation, *but it was the very thing she couldn't do.* If anyone realized how terrified she was, things would be worse, and she'd do something she couldn't undo.

The mirror before her, high on the wall, reflected an image of her tall, gracious form in a dress of clinging red silk. A magnificent body, like that of a crouching panther. But her face—her extremely odd, asymmetrical face, with a high forehead under a helmet of black hair, thin, arched eyebrows and small, twitchy snub nose above a heart-shaped mouth—looked exhausted. Her face, whose impassive mask she knew, had betrayed her this time, and had twisted in a spasm of terror that made it hateful to her.

She would gain control of herself whatever the cost.

She looked around at the ladies seated on sofas and armchairs along the walls and tried to smile. By this time, all three showrooms were full. Milan's very best clients, the richest—truly the ideal clients for a great fashion house—had accepted her invitation, and now she was about to faint in that very spot, in front of everyone…

She found the strength to shake off the fear that was paralysing her and move towards the nearest door, which led to the corridor.

At that moment the loudspeaker announced the return of one of the three models.

"Number 2449… 2-4-4-9… dressed for evening in black leather embroidered with black pearls in the form of a horse-chestnut leaf…"

The model walked through the door Cristiana been heading for and paraded in front of the assembled ladies, accentuating the artificial rhythm of her steps until she was practically dancing. On her painted face she wore a vacant smile, and her hands were extended in an absurdly showy gesture of offering.

Cristiana heard murmured comments. Everything was coming to her in a sort of feverish dream. The blood in her neck was pumping so rapidly that in her ears she heard the sound of the sea: thick, deep and persistent. She managed to get to the door and into the corridor.

Marta, in a formal gown of black silk short enough to reveal her knees, drew back to let Cristiana go by. She looked at her, curious, but the malice in her sharp gaze quickly changed to concern.

"Signora…" and she approached Cristiana, ready to support her.

"It's nothing! Watch the models, and above all, check every invitation."

"But Signora, you—"

"It's nothing, I tell you! It's too hot in here."

The director flinched as she watched Cristiana go. She ended up faintly shrugging her shoulders.

Cristiana marvelled that she'd been able to speak. As soon as she was in the lift, she sat down. Once again, a mirror appeared to confront her with her own image. She could think now. What a shock she'd had! But was it possible? Was she fooling herself? A resemblance, yes, however extraordinary. It had to be a lookalike. Her mouth twisted in disgust. Disgust at herself. She had never, when confronted with danger, attempted to play tricks on her mind or delude herself. Even when she'd discovered the terrible truth about her husband, she'd borne the blow bravely, with calm and knowing courage. And she'd coolly prepared her escape. She'd resorted to hundreds of ploys in order not to betray her project, using them subtly and shrewdly. Her life had been at stake and she'd defended it. But now? She told herself she'd exhausted all her energies in that struggle, which was why she was now defenceless.

She was so lost in thought, so troubled, that she didn't notice the lift stopping, and she became aware of her sudden immobility only after several moments. When she saw the long white corridor stretched out before her, elongated by the tiled floor striped with black and the stylized herms facing each other on either side of the doors, she opened the lift gate, wondering why she'd fled up here. If the woman she'd seen in the showroom *really was* her, the one she feared—*and she was*—how could she hope to escape her? Anna Sage hadn't come to Italy alone, and she certainly wouldn't have attended this fashion show without knowing who Cristiana was. Russell would have sent her. Russell, who must also be in Italy. He'd evidently looked for her and found her.

Halfway along the corridor she stopped to enter her bedroom. This was why she'd fled—to take refuge in solitude, and because she absolutely had to lie down, to throw herself on her bed.

Yet she couldn't, because the bed was occupied—by a dead body.

This time Cristiana O'Brian really did faint, and the thump of her body on the rug echoed dully down the corridor—without, however, toppling a single one of the eight fake marble herms.

2

Madame Firmino decided to spend the afternoon sunbathing. Sunlamp therapy is not the preserve of medical science; it's also one of the essential prescriptions for feminine beauty. Besides, it can be a pleasant distraction, and on that day, the 9th of March, Madame Firmino found herself with no better or more pleasing way to pass the time.

Of course, she could have gone down to the salons to help out with the show of the new spring designs from Casa O'Brian. But she was the one who'd dreamt up those designs, the one who'd created them. They had been born before her eyes and she loved them. All the same, she was not fond of the women who came to see them, desire them and buy them. No, she honestly couldn't bear to think that one of her designs, conceived and created for the fluid, graceful limbs of their house model, might end up cockeyed over the fat and flabby, dumpy or even lopsided body of a woman who'd buy it just because she could afford to. Madame Firmino had been the artistic director at Casa O'Brian for a year now, and she'd made her name there, but she had never attended any of the fashion shows, where the new collections were flesh of her flesh, blood of her blood.

At three, after giving the final words of advice to the models and dressers, she went back to her rooms on the top floor of the building on Corso del Littorio, where the fashion house was located and she lived with Cristiana O'Brian. She began her sun cure at three-thirty. There wasn't any sun, at least not in her room, nor was there any sand or water. There was a soft, wide white rug, a huge, shiny, ultraviolet heliotherapy machine with a splendid round reflective dish, and to top it off, there was Dolores Delanay—known to all as Madame Firmino—in a yellow bathing costume with black stripes. She stretched out on the rug wearing white celluloid glasses with blue lenses and bronzed her shoulders and back under the machine's beneficial rays. Her striped costume made her look like some sort of strange animal, perhaps a cross between a chimp and a zebra. The zebra bit was for her costume, and as for the rest—platinum blonde hair, a small triangular nose, long chin and prominent cheeks, full lips and tiny eyes lost in the hollows under plucked eyebrows—she'd always had noticeably simian features.

After the forty-five prescribed minutes on her back, Madame Firmino was about to lie on the carpet so she could expose her chest and face to the regenerative rays. But a strange noise interrupted her just as she was turning over, a dull thud that actually shook the floor.

The woman leapt agilely to her feet and removed her protective glasses. Her cheeks and neck were slick with oil. Without thinking it through (since they could only remain firmly attached to their square columns), she thought one of the herms had fallen over. She went to open the door: all of them stood upright, unmoving, with fixed, faun-like profiles. A perfectly unruffled, pristine silence reigned. But she had clearly heard a thud.

In her rope sandals, Dolores stepped over the black and white tiles, shiny as mirrors. She carried on, her senses on the alert. When she got to Cristiana's room she saw that the door was open. In the middle of the floor was a large crimson stain: she instantly recognized Cristiana, lying there motionless. She began hurrying over to her when her gaze fell on the bed: a man lay there, his arms spread and legs splayed. His body was on a diagonal, as if he'd been thrown by a wave during a shipwreck. His wide-open eyes were glassy.

As a young girl, Dolores had been involved in a tragic fire in a large bazaar, and she'd seen many bodies asphyxiated by smoke or by the throng. They'd all worn that glassy-eyed stare and had looked like disjointed puppets. It therefore took her no time at all to see that this man was dead. But the disturbing question was: why had he been killed? There were so many questions…

Slowly and cautiously, she approached the bed. This was certainly a big mess, and on the day of a show, too. Why, though, had Cristiana O'Brian fainted in her room with a man's body on her bed when she should have been down in the showrooms watching the models and studying her clients' reactions?

Madame Firmino could now see, below those wide-open eyes, the rest of the dead man's face. A handsome youth, almost a boy, with fine, perfectly regular features. Long black hair thrown back and naturally a bit messy now. Dolores lowered her gaze to his clothing, all cut from turquoise fabric: a blue silk shirt, even a turquoise tie, heavy and opaque. The dead man's chubby hands seemed small and expressionless against the grey damask bedspread. Madame Firmino went back to studying his face. But of course. How had she failed to recognize him immediately? Probably because of that staring look. No one knew better than she, an artist, how the face and eyes can change one's appearance. She broke away from this unhealthy contemplation, which had kept her stunned and fascinated.

How had the young man died? And who could have wanted him dead? Cristiana? She rapidly turned and bent over the woman lying on the floor. She touched her cheeks, felt her wrists. Nothing but a swoon; Cristiana was undoubtedly still alive. Madame Firmino stood up. She felt a strange sense of pressure on her sternum, almost an urge to vomit. When it came down to it, her strength was limited, and she couldn't forget that her sun cure had been interrupted. It would be ridiculous if she fainted as well, like tin soldiers all lined up and falling, one after the other, when someone touches the first.

She stood, placed her hands on her hips and tried to breathe deeply. She had to act now. But what should she do? Go to the internal telephone? Call Marta, let the dressers know, have the secretary come up? That comical secretary in his ever-present black frock coat? Yes, she should at least do that, but it meant raising the alarm, throwing the whole place into a panic, admitting the scandal in the showrooms... In any case she had to take care of Cristiana first, revive her, hear her speak.

Cristiana wasn't moving. She was definitely breathing, but fairly weakly, intermittently and with the occasional gurgle. Madame Firmino's gaze returned irresistibly to the body. This time she saw... she saw the dead man's slender neck. How had she missed it the first time? Strangled. She tried to stifle it, but a suffocated scream came from her throat and she bolted into the corridor. There, the herms closed in around her, and she ran towards the lift. Incredibly, she suddenly remembered that she was in her black-and-yellow bathing costume, the one that made her look like a zebra. How she managed, miraculously, to go back to her room, grab a dressing gown and put it on, tie the cord round her waist and then jump back into the corridor, Madame Firmino never knew.

3

"Number 2472... 2-4-7-2... dressed for evening in white organdie with black lace insets..."

Irma left the models' room and crossed the corridor, her crinoline skirt opened umbrella-style around her legs. She took a step, watching the crisp rippling of the skirt. Yes, it was eighteenth-century. And now it would ripple gracefully before all those parakeets: black, yellow and green. It was the fourteenth dress she'd put on in less than two hours, and there were still at least two hours left. She was used to it, but what torture!

"Smile!" commanded Marta, who was watching her.

Irma smiled, opened her arms and lifted her palms outwards in that prickly gesture that said, "Don't touch—but do!", before walking into the showroom. Head down, Marta sighed and turned to go back into the models' room, but the door to the lift at the end of the corridor opened, and she saw the most unexpected vision: platinum hair in a mess, shiny red face, voluminous black dressing gown draped over her and tightened round her waist with a golden cord.

Madame Firmino! What the devil was the artistic director doing showing up in that costume in these showrooms packed with spectators? Obviously another of her oddities—but too dangerous this time for Marta not to try and stop it. She hurried towards her.

"Madame! Madame Firm—" She stopped. The expression on Madame Firmino's face and in her eyes was enough to cut off Marta's words at her lips. In any case, Madame Firmino spoke at once.

"Marta, something terrible has happened. Who's in there?" She pointed at the door to the administrative offices.

"Mr Prospero, Signorina Evelina, the girls..."

"Come with me!"

She grabbed Marta's arm and dragged her into the offices. They went through the first room, which was divided by a shiny wooden partition in which there were two windows: CASH and SUPPLIERS. A large matronly woman in a black dress—a hundred kilos of fresh flesh packed to bursting in silk and fine satin and squeezed into a whalebone corset—lifted her astonished round face from a large ledger and with small eyes sunken into her fat, watched them go into the director's office.

The room was huge and luxuriously furnished with a large rosewood desk, clear as a mirror, between two heavily curtained windows. There was another desk, quite a bit smaller, in the far corner, and a large number of armchairs. Next to each of these, a microscopic table with a silver ashtray and a crystal vase containing a yellow rose. A frail gentleman, all in black apart from a head of polished ivory, popped up like a jack-in-the-box from his desk in the corner. At first sight he resembled a porcelain knick-knack, one of those little men from Capodimonte or Copenhagen: so smooth, lustrous and glossy that even their dark clothes appear oddly dazzling.

"Ladies, oh, ladies! You frightened me! If you're looking for Cristiana, she's not here."

He noticed Dolores's black dressing gown and started, then dropped his gaze, only to be confronted by her bare feet in rope sandals. A profound and haughty disapproval could be read on his face.

"Madame Firmino, it is inconceivable that you should dare to—"

"Shut up, 'Oremus'!" Dolores shouted. "We have other things to do than listen to your tirades!"

She felt her energy suddenly completely restored. This silly little man had a talent for both exhilarating and irritating her whenever she saw him, but this time he had annoyed her so profoundly that the amusing nickname used by the dressmakers and models escaped her lips. "Oremus" went scarlet, and the veins in his forehead bulged. Fortunately for Madame Firmino, the incident had caused his glasses to slide off his nose, and he couldn't possibly explode at the foolhardy woman while he flailed around for them on the table.

"Damn!"

Marta looked at Prospero, then at Madame Firmino. "What's going on here?"

Dolores leant against the rosewood desk. "What's going on? Oh, just that—" she twirled her celluloid glasses by the arm "—it's just that there's a body on Signora Cristiana's bed. And the *signora* is lying on the floor in a dead faint."

Prospero uttered a sort of roar and emerged from behind the desk. He walked over to Dolores.

"You're mad!"

As for Marta, she contented herself with gently shaking her head. She'd been convinced of Madame Firmino's craziness for some time.

"Would you repeat that?" Prospero shouted. "Say something!"

"You are aware, Madame Firmino, that today is the day of the collection, and jokes are not always welcome," Marta sighed. "You must know that I'm too busy to waste time with your eccentricities."

Dolores was still perched on a corner of the rosewood desk, her dressing gown open to reveal her bare legs, so tanned they looked like brass. Marta looked at those legs and then at Signor Prospero, who was blinking rapidly.

"Go back to your sunbathing, Madame Firmino, and don't disturb those of us who are working."

"Do you think I wouldn't like to, Marta? Do you think it's actually advisable for me to have my treatment so rudely interrupted? The body is there; I didn't invent it. As for Signora O'Brian, I'm sure it's time to go and resuscitate her. I was on my own up there, and I won't try to hide it from you: the sight of that body upset me so much I couldn't do it. Even if it hadn't, I'm no good as a nurse and I wouldn't have known how to begin to revive her."

"A body? Good God, whose? We're all in here, and we're all alive."

Prospero stopped blinking.

"We're all here? Many people work here at Casa O'Brian. If you go upstairs, you'll find that one of us has been killed."

Marta blanched.

"Killed, you say? So it's actually true?"

Madame Firmino patted her dressing gown, searching for pockets it didn't have. She looked over at the desk, spotted a sandalwood box and reached out to take a cigarette from it.

"Give me a light, Mr O'Lary. I'm sure I'll faint too if I don't have a cigarette. It's not the least bit pleasant to see the body of someone who's been strangled."

"Oremus" extracted a lighter from the folds of his extremely snug frock coat. He watched the young woman as he held the flame before her face.

"How do you know he was strangled?" he asked suspiciously.

Dolores drew the smoke in hungrily. "He had two marks on his neck. Two ugly, obvious marks."

Marta made for the telephone on a small bookcase near Cristiana's armchair.

"What are you doing, Signorina?" Prospero squawked.

"I'm calling the doctor. What else would I be doing?"

"Don't you realize that if there's really a body we must call the police first?"

Marta stopped in her tracks.

"The police? With the showrooms packed with ladies?" The catastrophe had suddenly struck her. "But it would ruin us!"

"I have reason to believe that it would be rather serious if we didn't call police headquarters right away—in case it really is a body. And I'm asking you to follow me upstairs so we can check it. We can give Cristiana first aid while we wait for the authorities to arrive."

"Oremus" boldly headed for the door, with Marta trailing after him, groaning. As for Madame Firmino, she slid gracefully off the desk and went to collapse in an armchair.

"I really must get this oil off my face," she said to herself. And she started smoking again.

4

Cristiana came round unaided. The return of consciousness was accompanied by a dull ache in her left side just above the hip. She must have fallen on that side with the carpet, however soft and deep, failing to cushion her fall. It seemed she was returning from far away... her brain was foggy, without a ray of light. Only when she tried raising herself up on an elbow to ease the pain did she notice that she was lying on the ground, and at first she was merely surprised. But when she saw the bed and the dead man on it, her memory returned like a flash.

She jumped to her feet. Everything that had happened came back to her, clearly and in minute detail. It was all so unexpected, so troubling, right up to the discovery of the body on her bed, something that had been truly terrifying for her. But through some strange twist of fate—as if by collapsing in a faint she'd reached rock bottom, both physically and mentally—she was regenerated, regaining her sangfroid and her customary energy.

She sensed danger and traps all around her, and the awareness reawakened her fighting instinct, the impulse to protect herself. The sight of Anna Sage in the showroom had initially frightened her, but then convinced her to flee the showroom and take refuge in her own room. It had been childish, that escape, since to all appearances Anna had come solely to see and be seen. But Cristiana had then discovered the body of Valerio—in her room, on her bed.

He meant nothing to her. Just a loyal servant she'd met in Naples on her return from America. She'd taken him with her to Milan when he was barely more than a boy, and the young man was now twenty. He'd always been, for her, a loyal drudge, the slave she used *for everything she had to do in secret.* Her secrets... Just as when she'd first seen the body and fainted, her lips twisted in disgust, and a bitter taste rose to her throat. Her secrets... One needed them in order to live, no? And they'd poisoned her very life when she was starting out.

She looked at the dead man. Loyal drudge? She pursed her mouth in a tragic, cruel smile. *How and why had he been brought to her bed?* She recalled the sight of Anna Sage's face. Next to her there'd been another face, but behind an evanescent cloud of fog, its features confused and blurry. A man's face, the face of a man she'd loved and whom to all intents and purposes she still loved, even though he'd poisoned the very roots of her life. Had he come back to get her, to keep her, never to leave her again until death parted them? She shivered. Death had already entered her house; it was there beside her. *Why in her bed?* She knew that the police would be asking the same question before long. The judge, the inquest... and she'd left America because she didn't want to face the police! Yes, before long someone else would be asking: *Why is the body in that bed?* They'd question, rummage around, search. Above all, search. She'd have to be quick.

She walked over to the wardrobe and opened it. It was built in, and reasonably deep. She turned to glance at the door, which was still open. What if someone came in? Well, she'd have to risk it. No use wasting time closing the door. Besides, there was that body in her room. She couldn't shut herself up with that corpse lying there.

She pushed the clothes aside and climbed into the wardrobe. Reaching up, she felt around for a red lacquer box, a precious box with a rounded cover that sat on a beam jutting out from the wall. It was generally a good hiding place, but she knew from experience that the police always look inside wardrobes. In Cleveland they'd done just that, but they hadn't found anything, because Russell was too crafty to hide deeds or money in the house. She pushed her clothes back and closed the wardrobe door.

Cristiana held the box against her breast—the red lacquer was darker and shinier than her silk dress—and walked resolutely towards the other wall. She knelt by the hearth. A small electric stove stood between andirons surrounded by wood to give the impression of a real fire that had died out; there were radiators in that room as well in as the rest of the house. She pulled it towards her. There was a recess in the wall that stretched under floor level by about twenty centimetres: Cristiana put the box in the recess, covered it with a few pieces of wood and replaced the electric stove. She stood up. She had to act now, but how?

She had no time to think; the sound of the lift stopping at that floor made her jump. Someone was coming. She sat in a chair next to the door, far from the body, and collapsed. Quick steps echoed over the black and white tiles.

Prospero and Marta appeared at the door. Cristiana looked at them, her eyes blank, and let out a short sigh which sounded more like a sob. She held out her arm in the direction of the body.

"Valerio, Valerio… Someone's killed him."

Prospero, a black skittle with an ivory head, ran over to the bed, blinking rapidly. Marta hesitated momentarily. What did one do with someone who's fainted? Cold water? Smelling salts? Someone had told her you have to bend the patient's head down to make the blood run to it. She went to Cristiana and took her pulse; she certainly couldn't turn her over and let her head hang down.

"How do you feel, Signora?"

Cristiana looked at her dreamily.

"Why did someone kill that young man?"

"Be brave, Signora! It may have been an accident."

Prospero O'Lary's voice sounded agitated.

"It was no accident! He's really been strangled!" The little man bounced back from the bedside to the middle of the room.

"We must tell the police!"

Marta trembled. Cristiana closed her eyes.

"Do it now, Mr O'Lary," she murmured, opening her eyes. Only then did she see, sharply and clearly, an orchid on the chest of drawers. She hadn't noticed it before. And she certainly wasn't the one who'd put it in the small crystal vase.

5

At four-thirty a strange man arrived at the door of the building at Corso del Littorio 14, and stepped onto the red carpet. He definitely didn't look like one of the fashion house clients. Federico, splendid in bottle-green uniform with silver braid (one of Madame, the artistic director's designs), barred his entry.

"May I help you?" He looked as if he wanted to say, "You must have the wrong address."

The other man—tall, sturdy, smiling—regarded him benevolently. He looked like a rich peasant, with a red birthmark on his forehead, ruddy blond hair, a solid chest and the sweet and innocent expression of a man used to living in the open air.

"Isn't this the O'Brian Fashion House?" he asked in a tortured foreign accent.

"Indeed. But this isn't Tuesday!"

"Tuesday?" the gentleman asked in bewilderment.

"It's only on Tuesday that we receive suppliers, and in any case the service entrance is in via San Pietro all'Orto."

"I know," and he smiled indulgently, "but I'm not a supplier."

He took a blue envelope from the pocket of his chestnut-coloured overcoat, a great, bell-shaped garment with over-elaborate fastenings and stitching. He opened it to show the little card with its pierced white dove.

Federico couldn't believe his eyes. This man was a client, invited to the fashion show. But, he said to himself, he was definitely a foreigner, heaven only knew how rich. For Federico, rich foreigners at a fashion show could be as odd as they liked.

"Pardon me, sir. The catwalk show started an hour ago. Please!"

He walked the other man to the lift. When they got into the little compartment, the gentleman put a ten-*lire* note in his hand, smiling paternally. In his anxiety to close the lift door and gate, Federico tripped over the doormat and nearly dived headfirst into a window.

The man in the lift was still smiling. He pulled a case from his waistcoat pocket and took out a pair of large gold-rimmed spectacles, fitting the arms behind his ears. His appearance was more kindly and respectable than ever.

The lift door was opened for him on the first floor by Rosetta, who was wearing a white apron over a black dress. Wound around her head like a mouse's tail was a blonde plait. Her hands and feet were too large and her legs massive, the calf muscles showing through artificial silk stockings that shone as if a snail had left a layer of slime across them. She gave the new arrival the once-over and held out her hand to take his hat.

Clara, the senior employee, appeared at the door; she always assisted Marta during the first few days of a show, and she came in, cards and pencils in hand. She too was dressed in black silk and walked in wearing shiny silver leather sandals with cork soles and heels over ten centimetres high. She said nothing, but her look, lips pursed, rendered her face a picture of perplexity.

The gentleman slowly removed his overcoat, patting his jacket and waistcoat with a gesture of confident satisfaction. He then took the blue envelope from his overcoat and handed it to the young woman.

"Oh, don't think, Miss, that your designs could possibly interest me! But they do my sister, and I've come to pick her up."

Clara looked at the envelope.

"Mr Bolton?"

"Indeed, my dear girl, that is my name, John Bolton, and my sister is Miss Anna Bolton." He held out his hand for the invitation and the blue envelope and put them back in his pocket.

Clara watched him, nodded a welcome and led the way.

"Are you foreigners just passing through Milan?" And she said to herself that Evelina's idea of getting foreigners' names and addresses from the doormen at the grand hotels was beginning to bear fruit. Marta would have to take care of these two: who knew how much money they had!

"From Topeka," admitted Mr Bolton.

"Where?"

"Topeka. It's a city in Kansas, and Kansas is one of the forty-eight states of the Union in America. Topeka has the worst droughts, short, hard winters and long, torrid summers. We're foreigners, but we're not just passing through." When he laughed, his gold teeth shone as brightly as his glasses in the light from the lamps lining the long white hallway.

The young woman stopped at the door to the first of the three showrooms and waited for him to enter. The showrooms were connected by three wide arches, giving them the appearance of one enormous single room. Mr Bolton looked around curiously. He started for the door of the administrative offices, which was opposite the one to the showrooms, and was about to open it when Clara called him back.

"Mr Bolton! Mr Bolton! Where are you going?"

Smiling, he excused himself, but not before he'd had time to open the door and take a look inside. He closed it and headed for the showrooms.

At that moment the loudspeaker squawked: "*May is the month for clothes in brightly coloured fabrics and prints with floral allegories, feathers and underwater landscapes… such is the ravishing design that we now present, Number 2479… 2-4-7-9…*"

The American man stopped to listen. He shook his head indulgently.

"Fashion!" he murmured. "Today's women live to get dressed up. And they couldn't do anything more useful or pleasing as far as we men are concerned."

"Will you point out your sister, Mr Bolton?" Clara asked him. "I'll take you to her."

"Thank you," he whispered, and he began scanning the long row of armchairs and sofas full of women, all of them busy watching the model as she slowly advanced. One or two leant forward with their lorgnettes while others affected weary indifference, glancing through drooped eyelids. A black figure rose from the corner formed where the outer wall of the first showroom met the building's façade, and walked quickly to the door.

"Here's my sister," said Mr Bolton. "You needn't trouble yourself about us any more, Signorina."

Miss Bolton was undoubtedly striking, and had a pretty little tabby cat's face framed by a small black hat with a thick crêpe widow's veil. Her eyes, tilted upwards at the outer corners, had the clean lines of almonds, with glowing green irises. Her skin was milky-white, and her face pallid against her black outfit.

Tall and thin, Miss Bolton advanced with the ethereal weightlessness of a ghost, and Clara, who was struck by her appearance, noticed the quality and cut of her dress. It had to be from one of the great fashion houses. Bolton stepped back into the corridor followed by his sister. They exchanged several sentences and slowly made for the exit.

Just then the bell rang with the dull chirp of a tree frog. Rosetta ran to open the door. On the threshold was a man of pleasing and distinguished appearance, dressed with sober elegance. As soon as he stepped in he took off his hat and began to remove his gloves. He was followed by four other men considerably less elegant and pleasing than he, who did not remove their hats initially. Faced with the invasion, Clara began telling herself that this was truly a day of surprises. What's more, Cristiana and Marta had found a way of disappearing at exactly the right moment.

She approached the pleasant man while keeping an eye on the other four, who'd stopped to form a menacing barrier in front of the door.

"Didn't anyone tell you that you could have used the service stairs?"

"Indeed." The pleasing man, apparently in charge of the little troupe, turned and signed to one of the others, who strode forward and stood at attention. He was short and stocky, with legs too short for his sturdy body.

"Sir?" he said, removing his stiff hat, a fine example of old-fashioned headgear.

"Cruni, have the doorman show you the service entrance. No one must leave by it."

Sergeant Cruni disappeared downstairs.

"Sir, I said—" Clara exclaimed. She was beginning to feel strangely bewildered. But she didn't have time to finish protesting before Prospero O'Lary pranced in. He started for the sudden arrivals, pushing Clara aside with one hand.

"Police?"

"Inspector De Vincenzi."

"I am Prospero O'Lary, the administrative secretary of the business."

"I took your call, Mr O'Lary."

"Of course. But could I ask you to exercise the utmost discretion? Today is the first day of our show, and the showrooms are full. A scandal would ruin us. You do understand?"

De Vincenzi smiled at him affably. He understood. How many times in his career as an inspector had he had to understand!

"Where is the dead man?"

"Upstairs on the third floor. You might easily notice nothing."

"Because you can already tell me who the killer is?"

Prospero started. "Me?" He gasped. "How could I?"

"Because… Look, if he was killed in this building, I won't be able to allow anyone to leave before I've carried out the necessary investigations."

Clara looked at both of them, her eyes wide. A dead man… Behind her, Rosetta grabbed at her skirt. "Oremus"'s head had gone all red.

De Vincenzi felt sorry for the poor man. "Don't worry! And if possible, I will avoid disturbing the people gathered in the showrooms. My men can stay here at the entrance. No one will notice them."

A faintly ironic smile fluttered over his face: how could anyone believe that no one would notice their presence? He hung his hat on a hook.

"Sit down, all of you, and don't move from this room. No one must leave." He turned to the secretary. "That's an order, Signor O'Lary. Do what you need to do so that no one attempts to go against it and my officers don't need to enforce it. Now let's go."

Prospero led the way. They passed Clara. De Vincenzi observed everything around him. He saw the Boltons standing in the corridor and Anna's green eyes struck him, as did her crêpe veil. For his part, Bolton stared at De Vincenzi, no longer smiling. When the men had disappeared into the lift, the American glanced at his sister and nodded imperceptibly towards the showrooms. The two of them slowly went in.

"*Even seaside fashion betrays some interesting nineteenth-century influences, seen through the multifaceted crystal of our century. Notice, for example, the original design we present here...*"

Through the crystal lenses—neither multifaceted nor graduated—of his gold-rimmed spectacles, Mr Bolton could in fact see a bathing costume with an extremely short skirt and a clinging bolero that barely fastened under the breast of the beautiful model.

"What have you done, Anna?" he whispered without moving his lips.

"I saw her."

"Did she recognize you?"

"I think so."

"It smells like something's burning in here…"

Anna Bolton sat down in an armchair and her brother took a seat beside her.

6

De Vincenzi saw the body, Cristiana and the orchid. By now he was used to seeing bodies and women—how many inquests had he racked up, each with at least one body and always lots of women?—but less used to seeing orchids, though he loved them quite a bit more.

So he stopped to look at the flower for longer and with greater pleasure. An unnatural flower made of flesh, born from rotting slime, grown in a tropical atmosphere. He sensed the woman looking at him, her gaze heavy, suspicious and enquiring. He was particularly well acquainted with the look women have when they find themselves in a frightening situation and are forced to defend themselves. He knew that a sudden, unexpected question can take a man by surprise, but a woman, never. Lying and distraction come easily to women; their deviousness is automatic.

He lifted his eyes from the orchid and looked at the body, moving so quickly that he bumped into Prospero O'Lary, who had come up beside him without his noticing. Prospero teetered and stumbled before steadying himself and finding his balance.

"Pardon me," he muttered, red in the face. He pushed his glasses up his nose.

De Vincenzi stood over the bed. He could see for himself that the young man had been strangled, but he needed to know much more. However, he could do nothing but wait for the doctor, who had been called and would get there whenever he got there—at his own convenience.

How long had the victim been dead? Had he really been strangled? It wasn't that he doubted it, yet the young man bore no other visible traces of beating or injury: he was healthy and strong enough to have put up a defence. Was it possible that he'd been killed without a struggle? His face was both handsome and common, with an air of cynical, insolent effrontery even after death.

"Who is—or rather, who was he?" he asked without turning round, still studying the dead man's clothing. It was costly and pretentious, silk, with a gaudy handkerchief tucked into his breast pocket.

"Valerio Tardini," said O'Lary.

"Oh, no! just *Valerio*. You only need to call him Valerio." Cristiana's voice resonated musically, full of melodic undulation, though it was thrumming with suppressed anxiety.

De Vincenzi left the bed and went over to stand beside Cristiana, who was still sitting.

"Am I to understand, Signora, that this man meant something to you?"

Cristiana couldn't raise her eyebrows in surprise—they already formed two black arches in the middle of her forehead. But her eyes widened.

"Meant something? Oh, no! Valerio was nothing to me. He didn't mean anything to anyone. He was my personal secretary, having been my waiter and then my errand boy. He belonged to me, belonged to the O'Brian Fashion House."

"I see," De Vincenzi said suavely. "He belonged to you, like an object, or a cute pet."

Cristiana scrutinized him. "You're a police inspector, aren't you?"

De Vincenzi bowed his head.

"How did you know that he belonged to me in just that way?"

"I think that's what you wanted me to understand. But why was he killed, and here on your bed? Isn't this your room?"

"My room, Inspector, and that's my bed. Why he was killed, I have no idea, unless someone did it just so I'd find him on my bed!"

Should he interpret her reply as a confession or a complaint? Too soon! He mustn't jump to conclusions. If ever there were a case that couldn't be rushed, it was this one. De Vincenzi sensed snares and danger as a diviner senses water, and he'd felt them from the moment he'd walked into the building. To complicate things further, there was a general air of suspicion, enough to give one the shivers. He remembered having had the same impression many years before, when he'd been embroiled in the mystery at The Hotel of the Three Roses during an awful, nightmarish and interminable evening of bodies.

He made a show of giving no weight to her words.

"Will you tell me how events took place?" And he turned away, as if he hadn't put the question to Cristiana. It was then that he noticed another woman in the room. Marta was in fact leaning against the wall near the wardrobe, eagerly watching, listening and hoping to understand the thinking behind his words and actions. This was someone new to him. On the way to the lift, Prospero O'Lary had spoken only of Cristiana O'Brian and the dead man.

"Events? *But there were no events,* Inspector, or at least there was only one. I came up to my room, saw the body and…" she smiled, both pitying and excusing herself, "and I think I fainted. It's never happened to me before, Inspector. I beg you to believe me when I say it's never happened before."

"I believe it, Signora. How long were you away from your room?"

"Well—for a long time. Since this morning. My life takes place downstairs, on the first floor, in my office and the showrooms. I come up here during the day only to change my clothes, and at night, to sleep."

"What time was it when you came up today?"

"Oh, I know very well. You policemen always want to know the exact time everything happened. As though anyone who does anything keeps track of time with a stopwatch! However, it must have been four, Inspector. I say four because the fashion show began at three-thirty with the models, and I was there."

"So you came up to change your dress?"

She didn't hesitate. She lied immediately.

"Exactly. I was tired of seeing myself in that red dress. There are a lot of mirrors downstairs."

"Do you live alone on this floor?"

"There's Madame Firmino."

"Madame?"

"Firmino. She's my artistic director, a French woman from Antibes."

"Was she with you in the showrooms?"

"No, that was exactly where you wouldn't have found her."

Marta finally pulled herself together.

"Madame Firmino came up to her room at three. She never attends our fashion shows. She says it's a nauseating spectacle for the person who's created the designs. A little after four, we bumped into her downstairs. She was in her bathing costume, barely covered by her dressing gown."

She waited for De Vincenzi to interrupt, but he contented himself with a nod, as if the matter appeared entirely natural to him. So Marta explained.

"Madame Firmino takes a sunlamp cure—UV-ray therapy."

"Interesting."

"Do you think so? Well, she heard a thud in her room, rushed in here and found Signora Cristiana O'Brian in a faint on the floor and—and—" She stopped and pointed to the body.

"I see."

"At least, that's what she told us," Prospero O'Lary added. "But it's absolutely true that she was taking a sun cure."

"You gathered that from her costume?"

"I deduced it from the fact that her face was covered in oil," "Oremus" affirmed in disgust.

"You can't argue with that."

Yes, that might have been so. At least, *that was how it looked*, an impression the killer wanted to create. But, thinking about it carefully, that impression did nothing but distance him from the killer.

"And Valerio?"

"What about him?" Cristiana asked.

"Where should he have been at that time?"

"Wherever he wanted! Valerio didn't have a schedule, or even somewhere specific to be. The room he slept in is on the second floor beyond the atelier. He could come and go as he pleased. I needed him only rarely, and in any case I certainly wouldn't have needed him today, the day of the show."

"And not one of you saw him today?"

"He came to see me at eleven and asked for something to do. I didn't have anything for him so he went off. I didn't see him again from that point on."

De Vincenzi addressed Marta. "And you are?"

"The director."

"Did you see Valerio today?"

"I saw him."

"Where?"

"Where I always see him—in the models' room. He spent his time with those girls since they usually have nothing to do."

"What time was it?"

"Two. Because I'd forbidden him to go into that room and the models had a lot to do today, Valerio escaped as soon as he saw me."

"So he was still alive at two. Did Valerio often come up to this floor?"

There was a quiet pause. For the first time, De Vincenzi felt that his question had met with some resistance. Up to then he had been shadow-boxing.

"I told you he was free to go wherever he wanted." Cristiana's tone was cold and sharp.

"But what reason could he have had for coming here? To your room, for example?"

Prospero O'Lary squirmed, but Cristiana stopped him.

"No one ever knew what was going on in that boy's head, not even me. He had a devious mind. *And anyway, Inspector, who says he was killed in this room?"*

"Of course." De Vincenzi looked at the orchid. "Are you an orchid lover, Signora O'Brian?"

Cristiana trembled visibly.

"I detest them. *That flower, too, was brought to my room without my knowledge. Just like the body!"*

7

The door to Cristiana's room was still open and a very tall man appeared at the threshold. He was extremely thin and lugubrious. He had a leather case under his arm and wore a wide black hat with a sloping brim. His black bow tie sat under his overcoat, which was buttoned up to the collar. He glanced around the room, looking first at the body and then at the people standing around it. He took off his hat and stayed where he was.

It wasn't hard to guess that he was the doctor.

"Come in, Doctor."

The young man's horsey face lit up as if the immediate recognition had thrown him a lifebelt.

"I came as soon as I heard." And he stepped into the room.

His shyness disappeared once he was in the presence of the body. They all watched him as he threw his wide hat on the floor, put his leather case on a chair and bent over the dead man. They followed closely as he took one of the hands by the wrist, lifted the arm and let it fall back down.

He turned to De Vincenzi. "Can I move him?"

"As you wish, Doctor. But tell me first whether his position seems normal to you for a man who was killed in this room. Let me explain myself. Do you think he fell from the killer's grasp like that and then died on the bed, or was he brought in and dropped there *after* he died?"

"Hmm," said the doctor, and he took a second look at the body.

Valerio's torso lay on top of the bedspread, at a slight diagonal, his head bent towards one shoulder and his legs dropped over the side of the bed; his feet nearly touched the floor. The grey damask bedspread was smooth and showed no trace of a struggle. Moreover, Valerio's arms were thrown apart and his hands were open.

"Did you study him, Inspector?"

"Naturally."

"And what have you concluded?"

"Given that one can't strangle someone else without a struggle, I feel that the body is too well composed to have been killed where it was found. The bedspread has no creases on it other than the ones made by the body."

The doctor shook his head.

"You're mistaken, Inspector."

De Vincenzi was shocked. "So you'd say that there had been a mortal struggle here on this bed?"

"Certainly not! That isn't your error. Naturally, you haven't had to digest the works of Gross, Niceforo, Filomusi-Guelfi and Nysten, so you're unaware of experiments that have established how a superficial trauma to the upper laryngeal nerve can result in sudden death. There are many cases of sudden or rapid death caused by a blow to the throat, even when it's not very forceful or leaves no sign."

"But the signs are here!"

"Indeed"—the doctor pointed to the victim's throat—"there are several obvious abrasions and bruises indicating that this poor man was grabbed by the throat and squeezed till he suffocated. But the semicircular abrasions made by the outer edges of the fingernails are missing. No, believe me, Inspector, in this case the clutch was calculated and pressure was applied immediately to the lethal spot. This young man died in a few short seconds and you'll see the autopsy will bear me out, since they won't find any rupture in the muscular fibre, much less a rupture of the intima or the hyoid bone."

"So you allow that he might have been killed on this bed?"

"No. I rule out the bed. But there's another reason. If death really occurred instantaneously, the pressure had to be equally rapid. Does this strike you as the normal position of a man surprised by an attack? Clearly not. The body is lying here as we see it because it was thrown there after death. Rather than thrown, placed. But I don't know where he was killed. It could have been in this room or some kilometres from here, supposing that whoever murdered him was sufficiently robust to have carried a weight like that for some time."

Yes, the young doctor's conclusions were perfectly sound and logical. Valerio could have been killed on Cristiana O'Brian's bed or somewhere else. However, De Vincenzi had a strange feeling that he hadn't been killed in that room. A feeling, however, for now completely lacking any logical explanation. The killer might have taken Valerio by surprise in the room or come up behind him, and then thrown him on the bed—in which case there would be no need to look for signs of a struggle.

"How long has he been dead, in your opinion?"

The doctor smiled fleetingly, with the immediate effect that his face seemed even more funereal.

"We don't have any symptoms of rigor mortis here, and since that appears from three to six hours after death depending on the subject and ambient temperature, I would say that this young man expired around three hours ago, definitely not more than six. One takes the internal temperature and then calculates by the degree to which the body has cooled. As a general rule, the temperature of a cadaver drops progressively one degree Celsius every hour, from 26 degrees, which is the temperature at which death occurs. But this sort of estimate is fairly unreliable and quite often wrong. No, Inspector, content yourself with knowing that this man was definitely alive six hours ago and could even have been alive for three hours after that."

De Vincenzi took his watch out: it was ten past five. Marta had seen Valerio at two, so presumably the young man had been strangled between two and four, when Cristiana found the body—as long as it really was the owner of the O'Brian Fashion House who'd found the body.

The doctor picked up his hat and leather case.

"Are you sending him to the morgue right away?"

"As soon as possible."

"In that case, you have no further need of my work."

He bowed slightly towards the dead man, again, more definitively, towards the inspector, and glanced at the bystanders. Then, crossing the room in a couple of long strides, he vanished into the corridor, his pedantic and monotonous voice echoing through the anxious silence of the four people huddled around the body.

The first to break that silence was Prospero O'Lary, in a voice so hoarse it sounded like the creaking and groaning of ice as it cracks.

"I would ask you please, Inspector, not to act on your suggestion."

Still gazing at the orchid, De Vincenzi roused himself.

"Which one?"

"That of having the body removed immediately. The stretcher would have to pass through the showrooms—which are full of ladies… clients—first empty, and then with its grim burden. Not to mention the panic it would cause the dressmakers and the rest of the staff."

"You're forgetting, Prospero: there's a service stairway," Signora O'Brian said coldly.

De Vincenzi noted that Cristiana had moved her armchair slightly so she wouldn't have to keep looking at the body, and he thought to himself that this woman for whom Valerio was nothing more than a pet had a strong desire to see his macabre remains disappear.

She walked over to the bed, lifted a corner of the damask bedspread and pulled it over the corpse.

"I have nothing against that, Signor O'Lary, particularly since the investigating magistrate has yet to arrive and give the authorization. But Signora, you spoke of the service stairs."

"Yes. They start from this floor, communicate with the corridors on the other two floors and end in the small courtyard on the via San Pietro all'Orto side of the building."

"Is the door to via San Pietro all'Orto left open all the time?"

"No, it's always closed. You need the key to get in. It's left open while the staff are arriving and departing and also on Tuesday, when we receive suppliers."

"Who has the keys to that door?"

Cristiana turned questioningly to Marta, who said, "Signora O'Brian, me, Madame Firmino, Signorina Evelina and... Valerio also had one. And of course Federico, the doorman."

"So the service entrance was closed today?"

"Especially today. With all the people filling up the show-rooms, there's always the risk that some stranger could use that entrance to get in and mingle with the invitees. We don't have private security like the other fashion houses, but we worry no less about our designs. You may not know, Inspector, that it's possible to steal a very valuable design just by looking at it."

De Vincenzi smiled at her cordially.

"I'm aware of that, Signorina, and so much so that I'd ask you to take me to meet your Madame Firmino, the creator of your designs. I understand that she stayed upstairs in the offices."

"She did."

"Well, take me to the offices."

"But Inspector, I've told you that Madame Firmino is in her bathing costume, with her face all oily!" "Oremus" broke in almost violently.

"Oh, don't worry, Signor O'Lary. I've seen women with their faces covered in aromatic oils before."

8

Cristiana wouldn't look at the bed, now in such strange disarray. Valerio's body made a lump under the bedspread. As soon as Marta and the inspector left, she deliberately turned her armchair to face the dresser with the orchid on top of it. Behind her and between her chair and the body, Prospero O'Lary stood staring at the door the other two had just gone through. Rays of March sun were coming through the ivory silk curtains and glass of the window, cold but clear and razor-sharp.

"I wonder..." he murmured.

Cristiana's voice rose up from the back of the tall armchair, so low and strangled that it seemed to be issuing from the depths of some strange altar.

"I'm wondering the same thing, Prospero. It's a very serious question, and I don't have an answer for it."

Prospero started.

"It's always painful—and dangerous to ask oneself questions. But I'm wondering what Madame Firmino will say to the inspector. That dear young woman has a screw loose. She might introduce some unexpected and unpleasant complications."

"No complication will be as unpleasant as the presence of that orchid in the vase, O'Lary. Do you know the symbolic significance of the orchid, Prospero?"

The little man hopped over to the dresser, looked at the flower and turned to Cristiana.

"I don't know any apart from that of the aster—the symbol of Christ."

Cristiana shrugged.

"If only Christ could really help us… Who would kill Valerio? Who would bring his body and that orchid to my room, O'Lary?"

"Valerio was destined to end that way."

"Because he was corrupt—is that what you're saying?"

"Because he played with fire."

Cristiana shot a look at the fireplace, and the look wasn't without apprehension.

"I don't understand you, O'Lary," she said sternly.

"Oremus" blinked and held up a hand to calm her.

"It doesn't matter, Cristiana. In fact, forget I said it. You know I sometimes talk nonsense. Over there, too, in Portland, when you turned to me to help you escape—to free yourself from Russell Sage…"

Prospero's voice had become shrewd, insinuating, perhaps a bit ironic. Cristiana paled, and her eyes shone cold and menacing.

"O'Lary!" she hissed. "It's dangerous to talk about him." She shivered and then abruptly let out a short laugh. "Do you know what happens to people who mention the devil?"

Prospero adjusted his glasses. "What are you trying to say, Cristiana?"

"Just what I said. If you saw Russell appear in front of you, what would you do?"

"In fact he has already appeared. I recognized him immediately just a short while ago, down the corridor. Did you know he was coming? Have you seen him?"

"I saw his sister, that dreadful sister-in-law of mine."

"Is Anna Sage in Milan as well?"

"At this moment she's in our showrooms. When I recognized her, I didn't know what to do except get out of there, so I ran up here, where I found Valerio's body and the orchid. What do you make of all this, O'Lary? Did you know that every time Russell came back home after one of his trips—which I thought were to do with his job as an insurance salesman, and instead were all about meeting up with his gang to raid banks—did you know that he always brought me an orchid? Flowers are his weakness! Just like books, pictures and stamps. A great collector, my husband. And a pure spirit, so pure that he made the innocent Ileana love him and marry him."

The painful sarcasm in her words trailed off in a sob.

"It's impossible," Prospero murmured.

Cristiana shrugged once more.

"The body is there… and the orchid… *And I am Ileana, even if my name is now Cristiana O'Brian.*"

Prospero looked at the bed.

"It's impossible," he repeated. "How could he have got in here—and why would he have killed Valerio?"

Cristiana replied to his question with another one.

"Perhaps he doesn't know yet that you came with me—that you're here with me. Why don't you go while you still have time, O'Lary? Russell isn't a forgiving sort of man. If he's been looking for me and has found me, he must have a plan, and Russell Sage's plans are always dangerous. Like a stick of dynamite!"

Prospero adjusted his glasses. "Russell Sage thinks I'm dead," he said slowly. "He won't recognize me, and if he does he'll think he's seeing a ghost."

"As you wish." Cristiana got up. "In any case, it's necessary to do something now."

"What are you going to do?"

"That's what I've been asking myself since I came to. What can I do? I can't even escape now. If it was Russell who killed Valerio, he did it to force me to stay."

There it was. It was a possible theory. The body had been put in her room in order to compromise her and prevent her leaving. It seemed clear and logical to her, and she took heart. She liked clear and logical situations. And if Russell had ultimately just wanted to keep her from getting away again… But how had he managed to get into the building?

"What do you think, O'Lary?"

"Yes," the little man murmured without conviction. "He *might have* killed him for that reason; but I still don't see how he could have done it. Was it only today that you saw Anna Sage?"

"Yes. She must have had an invitation in order to get in, otherwise Marta or Clara would have stopped her. How could she have got one?"

"Oremus" fluttered his eyelids and his face lit up.

"Maybe Valerio's death can explain it!"

Cristiana wrinkled her forehead.

"Do you think Valerio betrayed me?"

"Valerio always needed money, and he'd never have imagined that Russell P. Sage would settle the score like that—" and he pointed to the bed with a sardonic grin.

They heard a step in the corridor. A slow, deliberate tread, advancing confidently and inexorably. The sound was all the more strange to their ears for having arisen so suddenly. It was immediately obvious that it came not from the stairs, but from the corridor itself.

Paralysed with fear, Cristiana looked at the door, her eyes wide. The waiting went on for several seconds as the step slowly advanced. At last the earnest, smiling figure of John Bolton appeared in the doorway.

His voice was warm and cordial. "You're alone, Ileana my dear! It's just how I hoped to find you."

The terrified woman looked around. Indeed, she was alone. Prospero O'Lary had simply vanished.

9

Marta opened the door to the administrative offices and, after a quick glance inside, stood aside.

"Madame Firmino is still there."

De Vincenzi sent a reassuring smile Evelina's way. Her small eyes were fixed more firmly than ever on the ledger. The mature, fat lady's face, so serene, so sweetly pink, immediately inspired the inspector's trust.

"Has the *signora* been in this room for long?"

Marta looked first at Evelina and then at De Vincenzi.

"Of course! Signorina Evelina is always in the office at two."

"I eat in the building, in the employees' cafeteria."

The earnestness shining through her words convinced De Vincenzi that Evelina would be the ideal, truthful witness, if indeed she had anything to say. He went to stand by her desk.

"Lots of work, eh?"

Evelina put her hands palms down on the sheets, where she was filling in figures across five columns, and fixed her gaze on the intruder with less kindliness. As far as she was concerned, it wasn't done for strangers to take an interest in her accounting: a firm's books are secret and sacred.

"Are you the administrator, Signora?"

"Signorina," the spinster corrected, lowering her gaze. Then, her voice stronger, "I keep the books, and sometimes also the petty cash. But the administrator is actually Signora O'Brian, aided by Signor O'Lary."

"I see." De Vincenzi leant familiarly against the desk, keeping his gaze from the sacred account books. "And have you seen Valerio today, this afternoon?"

The unexpected question caused Evelina's calm face to blanch.

"Valerio? What does Valerio have to do with me?" She turned to Marta as if imploring her to intervene.

The director stood just outside the administrative offices, holding the door ajar. In answer to Evelina's silent, alarmed plea, she lifted her shoulders in a sign of powerless resignation.

"The gentleman is a police inspector."

De Vincenzi moved away from the desk. Nothing was more important than winning Evelina's trust and goodwill.

She stiffened immediately into a solid block of frozen flesh. Her cheeks trembled slightly and her chest heaved under her silk bustier, which was too tight.

"Police? Why the police?" Her eyes flashed with ill-humour under heavy, fat eyelids. "I always thought that bad boy would meet a sorry end."

"He ended up terribly, in fact, Signorina. Simply put, someone strangled him."

This time the blow hit hard. Evelina swayed and collapsed like a young calf under the mallet.

"But I saw him. I saw him and he was alive!" she whined.

"What time did you see him, Signorina?"

The pale woman was trembling all over.

"A glass of water," she begged in a faint voice.

Her eyes were wide with alarm. Marta ran and De Vincenzi grabbed her arm.

"She has a bad heart."

"Give her some water."

Marta ran towards the administrative offices and disappeared through the open door. De Vincenzi grabbed the woman's hand and gently and repeatedly slapped her back. She seemed to be coming to. The colour was returning to her face and her cold sweat was over.

"Oh!" she sighed, and looked at De Vincenzi in confusion. "How horrible!"

De Vincenzi continued to pat her, feeling as though he were smacking a baby.

"Don't think about it, Signorina. We'll talk about it later, calmly." At the sound of Marta's returning steps he moved away from Evelina.

"We'll speak about it *alone*."

Evelina's eyes flashed with fear, and De Vincenzi was convinced that she would be of great help to him—if only he could get her to speak.

"Give her something to drink, Signorina. Spray some water in her face, and take her to the window so she can get some fresh air. I'm going to have a word with Madame Firmino."

He went into the administrative offices before Marta could respond. Dolores hadn't moved from the chair, where she sat smoking. De Vincenzi saw her copper-coloured legs, oily face and a few stripes of her yellow-and-black bathing costume peeking out from under her dressing gown. Above all, he saw a sharp-featured, almost offensive face, and platinum-blonde hair. Madame Firmino's eyes had begun following him the moment he entered the room, and they never left him. It was evident that she knew, or intuited, who this competent gentleman advancing towards her was, and it was equally clear that she was on the defensive. The inspector threaded through the chairs and small tables and bowed to the young woman.

"I've come to speak with you about fashion and design, Madame Firmino. I know how talented you are in this area."

Dolores wasn't going to be tricked, though this was the most astonishing preamble she could ever have imagined.

"Are you investigating Valerio's death?"

De Vincenzi waved away this clarification.

"Working in an environment you don't understand is quite difficult, Signorina. Will you help me?"

"Did they tell you I was the first one to find Cristiana in a faint and Valerio dead on the bed?" She threw her finished cigarette into a crystal goblet on the little table and took another from the sandalwood box, which she had appropriated.

"Do you have a light? Since I've been in here I've had to light each one off the other because I left my room without bringing any matches." She smiled. "And no cigarettes, either, for that matter. The ones I'm smoking are Cristiana's. That will teach her to faint when she sees a body."

De Vincenzi lit her cigarette.

"You don't smoke?"

"Rarely."

"Your brain doesn't need any stimulants?"

"I get them from observing details and people." He looked her straight in the face.

"Are you a police inspector?"

"That's right."

"I wouldn't like to be Valerio's killer. A police inspector who observes people and details is rather dangerous," she proclaimed, pulling the edges of her dressing gown over her legs. She put her hands on her knees and leant towards him.

"Question me. I'm ready."

De Vincenzi smiled again. However ready she was, Madame Firmino must have been aware internally that the man's every movement, each of his facial expressions and his reassuring smile projected a sense of calm indifference, as if he lent no weight to the matter of the dead man or his murderer. Yet despite telling herself that his behaviour was a trap, she was prepared to fall into it.

"Did you know Valerio well?"

"What do you mean by 'well'? I've been with Cristiana O'Brian for a year and I've known Valerio for a year. I saw him a couple of times a day, maybe more. I spoke to him rarely enough, and after he lost his initial illusions that he'd be able to court me, he never approached me unless forced to—if that's what you call knowing someone well. There was no intimacy between us; we weren't even compatible. Another level, another class."

"Why did Signora O'Brian keep him on?"

"Probably because he was useful to her."

"How?"

"Well, in the only possible way: serving her. Cristiana met him in Naples. He was already grown up, but ever the boy from the streets. She brought him here with her. Valerio had a certain intelligence and without a doubt a lot of cunning.

He attached himself to her and didn't let any possibility she offered pass him by."

"How did he get on with the staff?"

"Look, Inspector, the staff—as you call them—in this fashion house are all women. There are no men apart from Mr O'Lary and Federico, the doorman. So you can picture for yourself these relationships you're asking about. Valerio is a bit of a small-time Don Giovanni, and since he had unquestionable physical charms, he was lucky."

"Could a woman have killed him?"

"Well, why couldn't a woman have killed him? *But in Cristiana's room?*"

That was the exactly the problem: the place where the body had been found, and the added complication of the orchid. The problem was further complicated by the supposition that Valerio had been killed somewhere other than where he'd been put after his death.

"Tell me about Signora O'Brian, Signorina."

"Why don't you say: tell me about the last queen of Cambodia? What should I know about Cristiana? She's the owner of this fashion house, she's single—or seemingly so—and she's always very polite to me and to everyone. I create designs, invent dress styles, study colours, evaluate fabrics. I've too much work, don't you see, to concern myself with what has nothing to do with me. Cristiana is Romanian, or at least I think she has Romanian origins. She comes from America, and I've heard that she's been in Milan for two years. She seems to be widowed, or in any case she maintains that she is, and Prospero O'Lary maintains the same. He came with her from

America. She has money, maybe a lot, and this business is her first in Milan. If you go down to the showrooms, you'll find the best names from amongst the aristocracy and the wealthy. A dress from here never costs less than several thousand *lire*."

She tossed away her cigarette, started to take another and then halted. "I smoke too much! Over-stimulated. It makes me talk more than I should."

"Oh, you've told me enough, Madame Firmino. Absolutely enough, although you haven't talked to me about your designs. Is Signora Cristiana also a designer?"

Dolores smiled. She knew all too well how little Cristiana designed, and clearly what bad taste she had in clothing.

"Only one style, dear Inspector, and only two colours: tomato-red and first-Communion-blue; and when she happened to see a painting by Fragonard in Paris, you've no idea of the full skirts, long sleeves, scoop-neck corsets and on top of all that a gauzy scarf…"

"A bit outdated, yes?"

"Oh, no—it's a style one could still launch, provided it was updated, along with oneself. But as far as other people's clothes are concerned, Cristiana's stuck in a rut."

"But she must at least have some competence in constructing them?"

"Ask Marta about it. She's had to plead with her not to set foot in the atelier."

"I see. She's interested in fashion as an industry. She's got good business sense."

Madame Firmino's smile was the picture of spite. "No, she's not lacking business sense."

De Vincenzi got up. "When did you last see Valerio today?"

"I don't think I actually saw him, but I heard him. I heard his annoying whistle, which almost always preceded him as he came through the corridor my room's on."

"What time was that?"

"Oh, God, Inspector! I didn't look at my watch. But it must have been after two-thirty, because I came up to my room at two-thirty to dedicate myself to my treatment."

Cristiana had discovered the body just before four. De Vincenzi saw a piece of white paper on the rosewood table. He picked it up and held it out to Madame Firmino with a gold pencil he took from his waistcoat pocket.

"May I ask you to draw a design for me?"

She looked at him, astonished.

"A dress design?"

"I'm not asking that much. I just need you to draw me a plan of the third floor of this building."

"Oh."

She hesitated, then shrugged her shoulders. Setting the paper on the small table, she covered it rapidly with lines first, then words.

"You could have had anyone draw this for you... so it might as well have been me."

De Vincenzi studied the paper.

"Thank you for writing down what each room is used for. It's all perfectly clear, except for this last room." He pointed to a rectangle near the stairway at the end of the corridor.

"Oh, that! It's the room we call the 'museum of horrors'.

I was the one to christen it. That's where the mannequins are kept for all our usual clients."

"Excuse me, Madame Firmino, but I don't understand."

"Well, in order to work confidently and without troubling our clients to try things on too often, Marta orders a mannequin to a lady's measurements when she uses us regularly. It's a perfect replica of her body in wood and horsehair. Just imagine, Inspector, what horrors are kept in that room!"

10

"Surprise?"

"I knew I'd see you again fairly soon."

"Intuition?"

"Anna was here before you!"

"Deduction, then."

Silence. The man removed his spectacles.

"I have never known why spectacles, especially gold-rimmed ones, manage to give someone an air of respectability." Cristiana was now in complete control of herself. "Over there, too, you fooled yourself into thinking that your appearance was perfectly respectable. No one fell for it—apart from me."

Russell P. Sage smiled disappointedly. "As it happens, the G-men were at my heels! But here it's another story. Here I'm John Bolton, a rich industrialist from Chicago, and I have no intention of robbing any banks. I'm developing an idea for starting up a toy factory."

"Just like in Portland."

He interrupted her with a wave of his hand. "Quiet! The Ultra Products Company is over. I won't be making any more toy animals or tin soldiers. Different strokes for different folks… I'm dreaming of some little cars… they'll be masterpieces. I'll make the children of this country happy when I produce them in series. The market will be flooded with Bolton automobiles."

Cristiana stiffened. "What do you want from me?"

"Oh, nothing you can't give me. I want your love."

Cristiana laughed, a vibrant, tinny laugh that was hard on the ears. "You've killed off any possibility of my loving you, Russell."

"I'm not trying to gloss over what I did to you, Ileana. I shouldn't have got carried away."

"You think that's your only fault?"

"Of course! I didn't have the right to drag you into my mess and you did well to get away while you could. You were very perceptive when you said that the break-in at the Caledonia National Bank in Danville would be my last exploit and that I'd be appearing in court in Rutland." His voice suddenly dropped, but the words hammered on. "But you shouldn't have lost your faith in me, Ileana. I gave you too much for you to doubt me." He'd grown excited. "Oh, no, you shouldn't have been hoping you'd never see me again!"

Cristiana pursed her lips.

"There's nothing left to say. Not a thing more I can do for you, Russell Sage! You can't get me back, even if there *is* a body lying under my bedspread."

Russell followed her gaze and noted the dishevelled bed, with a dead man's feet sticking out from under the damask.

"Is that why the police are here? And just when I came up here to help you!"

He watched her. His face had turned dark and a vein near the birthmark on his forehead was pulsing and bulging. As he studied her, he drummed the fingers of one hand on the opposite fist. He appeared to be working hard at his reflections. All at once he shook himself.

"A trap, eh?"

He looked at her again, but this time in admiration. "You are a force to be reckoned with! I didn't appreciate you as I should have." He put his spectacles back on. "I'm not worried about your telling the police who John Bolton really is. It would be too dangerous for you, and actually not at all for me. I'll leave this building calmly, Ileana. But we'll see each other again."

He backed up to the door, taking small steps and staring at her. Suddenly he darted into the corridor and headed confidently for the service stairs, which he descended quickly and lightly, arriving at the first floor without anyone hearing his tread. A short time later he arrived in the showrooms just as the loudspeaker was announcing the thirty-seventh outfit in the Cristiana O'Brian collection.

Cristiana remained motionless, staring at the door through which Russell had escaped. His sudden flight had surprised her. She'd been prepared to stand up to him, for a struggle, but everything had ended before it had begun. Well, his escape had been logical, an impressive example of quick thinking. Staying in that room and risking being surprised by the police would have been like confessing he'd killed Valerio.

But who had put the body on her bed? How had Russell known where to find her room and how to reach her without being seen by anyone? Was it possible that this wasn't his first time here? Her thoughts were confused. She had the sense that events around her had been taking shape over the last three hours, joining up and fusing into one giant bullet travelling through space like lightning—one that would inevitably hit her and explode in a horrendous uproar as it hit the ground. An uproar and a disaster that would sink her.

She jumped at a slight squeak. Immediately she turned to the wall with the wardrobe and dresser, since the sound seemed to be coming from that side of the room. The wardrobe doors looked to be only partially closed. Had she left them like that? She didn't have time to answer her own question before they opened to reveal Prospero O'Lary.

"You were in there!"

The little man climbed over the lower panel and emerged from his hiding place. He breathed a sigh of relief and adjusted the waist of his frock coat.

"Why did he go off so quickly?"

"He saw the body."

"Oremus" seemed perplexed.

"Of course," he burbled. Then, more clearly: "*He didn't kill Valerio!*"

"That's what he wants me to believe, in any case. How did he find my room?"

"You're forgetting that Russell knew how to rob a bank in broad daylight." He started for the door. "I must go back downstairs, and you'd do well to come down yourself. This room will be swarming with police before long. That inspector's way of doing things makes me uneasy—and the body even more so."

Cristiana watched him go. She heard his steps receding down the corridor as far as the lift, which opened and closed with its characteristic clatter. No. She would not go down. She looked at the orchid, then at the dresser and wardrobe. How ready Prospero O'Lary had been with his hiding place...

"Will you allow me to come in, Signora?"

Cristiana jumped like a startled panther.

"Ah, is it you, Inspector? You frightened me. Please, come in. Come in, of course."

De Vincenzi entered with an officer. Another could be seen in the corridor, looking with intense curiosity at one of the eight herms.

"Until the investigating magistrate comes and gives the authorization for the removal of the body, I'll have to put someone on guard in this room. Since all the necessities will be taken care of by this evening, you can provisionally go to your office, Signora."

A smile crinkled Cristiana's lips. "I was rather wondering why you hadn't already searched this room!"

"Do you think it would have been helpful if I had? Objects rarely speak in a criminal investigation, at least in the way most people mean. I never follow tracks or material clues. And that's why I'm so often mistaken!" he added, smiling at her cordially.

Cristiana looked about.

"I'd ask you only not to mess things up too much. My room won't thank you."

"I'll content myself with speaking to your maid instead, Signora. Would you have her come up if she's here?"

"Well of course she's here, Inspector! The service rooms and kitchen are on the second floor. I'll go and tell her."

She started to leave and the officer stepped aside to let her by, but she stopped at the threshold.

"Inspector, what precautions do you take against suspects here in Italy?"

"None, or almost none, Signora O'Brian. We're happy to wait until our suspicions are shown to be valid."

"Hmm. So you won't even have me watched?"

"Do you think you're under suspicion?"

"Well, you see, I'm the only one who could've had any reason to kill Valerio. That boy was becoming troublesome."

"If everyone who had some reason to kill really did kill, the ground would be strewn with bodies! Sometimes, the real killer does nothing but carry out someone else's desires... or those of many others, Signora. As for having you watched, I don't feel it's necessary. In any case, it won't be possible for you to leave the building."

The woman gave him one last look.

"I never thought the police in Italy had such... novel methods."

"Do my methods really seem so novel to you?"

"More than that, they seem dangerous. Goodbye, Inspector!"

"Don't be so sure, Signora," De Vincenzi said without irony. To his officer, he indicated one of the armchairs.

"Have a seat."

The man sat down. He was young, chubby and well groomed. He lifted his coat tails before sitting down.

"Is this the crime scene, sir?"

De Vincenzi began looking around; the wardrobe caught his attention.

"Call it the scene of the crime if you like."

"I don't see a body, sir."

"If you move you'll be touching it. You're sitting in front of it."

The officer turned round. He saw the bump made by the body under the bedspread, blushed and stood up at once. Smiling awkwardly at De Vincenzi, who was watching him kindly, he moved away from the bed and went to sit in a chair near the door, some way away.

"Are you afraid of the dead?"

"They give me the creeps, sir."

"It's the living who give me the creeps! You'll notice that with time." He opened the wardrobe and looked inside for a moment.

"For example, look at this. Someone—alive—has been in this wardrobe, and he didn't even bother to put the clothes back in their place!"

11

In Cristiana's wardrobe De Vincenzi discovered nothing other than lots of clothes and all kinds of lingerie. He saw the board sticking out a few centimetres from the back, which had to be a shelf. It was empty. Yet "Oremus"'s presence and movements through the clothes were obvious. Still, De Vincenzi couldn't draw from that any more than he'd stated: someone had hidden in that wardrobe, but he didn't know who. He supposed it could have been the murderer, and then almost immediately rejected that idea since it didn't square with his conviction that the crime had been committed outside of that room. The killer wouldn't have lingered in the room after putting the body on the bed, thinking it convenient to hide in the wardrobe. They might, if they'd been startled by the sound of approaching steps—Cristiana's, for example. But in that case they'd still be there amongst the clothes, since the room had been full of people ever since. Had it? What about when Cristiana had been lying in a faint on the floor—alone?

De Vincenzi shrugged. It was one of those questions logic couldn't resolve and which, even if resolved, wouldn't help him. The fact that someone had hidden in the wardrobe was significant in itself, as an identifying feature, and he actually needed to gather as many of these clues as he could in order to reconstruct the picture of the crime. Why, if it wasn't true, would Cristiana O'Brian have said that *the flower hadn't been there before the body*, and that she'd come across it when she'd made the macabre discovery of the body?

He sighed. How could one distinguish truth from falsehood in a woman's statements, and how could one find logic in her words and actions? Surely the whole story revolved around Cristiana.

"Don't leave here!"

The officer had been following De Vincenzi's movements in the room, and he nodded vigorously.

"Yes, sir."

"And don't worry about the body. The dead are harmless."

"I hope so, sir!"

De Vincenzi smiled and lifted the latch on the door between the wardrobe and the fireplace: it was the bathroom, a vast room with blue majolica on the walls and shining with nickel-plate and porcelain. The strong scent of creams, cologne and lavender lingered and enveloped him, warm, acrid and sweet. He recalled another observation he'd made previously: taste and smell are two senses that work in sympathy, because odours can offend the palate no less than the nostrils. But the reflection did nothing to dampen the irritation he felt in that heavy, humid air. A third sense immediately came into play, commanding all his attention. He saw something that interested him and induced him to cross the bathroom in order to reach the door opposite the one he'd entered.

A white-painted door, with a shiny handle and a small bolt. He bent down to look at the bolt, a short cylinder of nickel-plated steel that slid into rings fixed on two metal plaques screwed to wooden double doors. In order for the doors to open—both sides swung into the bathroom—the bolt had to be left off the latch. And that fancy gadget was shown to be of no practical use; it hung miserably from one the doors, attached to the wood only by a couple of loose screws. One of the two plaques—the one with the rings—lay on the floor in front of the doors. To all appearances, someone had forced the door and broken the latch in order to come through.

De Vincenzi lowered the bolt and pulled both doors towards him. The room he looked into was the very one he'd been seeking, the one he'd hoped to visit from the moment Madame Firmino had drawn the plan of the third floor for him, indicating this room as the "museum of horrors". The room was wide and rectangular, and the light coming from two windows immediately revealed its strange and grotesque contents. *The bodies of Cristiana O'Brian's clients were lined up against the walls.* Each mannequin was covered in grey canvas, and had on its breast a piece of paper bearing a name. Each balanced on a wooden foot with three pegs. There were all types: large, small, thin, bloated, with jutting breasts, lopsided shoulders, rounded stomachs—a horrifying anatomical display. And all those bodies, uniformly nude and grey, were missing their heads.

Other than the door leading to Cristiana's bathroom, the room had one that opened on the corridor; it must have been the one commonly used to enter it. At first, De Vincenzi walked slowly between the decapitated bodies, but he began to speed up. This inspection seemed macabre to him. He'd got as far as the end of the longest wall when he spotted an overturned mannequin and was compelled to stop. It was the only one in the row like that and clearly must have been bumped—either by accident or on purpose—to make it fall. He then noticed that the two on either side of it had been moved, and one of them was now leaning against the wall, with two of its foot pegs off the ground.

There had been a disturbance in that place, some kind of violent movement. Someone fleeing, who'd tripped and fallen on the mannequins, or an actual struggle: Valerio against his attacker? Had the young man been strangled in there, perhaps surprised from behind, grabbed by the throat, thrown about and beaten, first against the mannequin, which naturally fell over, and then against the wall?

De Vincenzi looked around at the floor and saw something shiny. He bent over to pick it up. A golden medallion, on one side of which were engraved the words: *San Siro Dog Track* and on the other a date: *8th February 1938—SVI E.F.* The ring from which it had hung was twisted open.

He put the medallion in his pocket and hurriedly left the "museum of horrors". It would be easy for him to find out whether the object had belonged to Valerio and to make up his mind once and for all. But until then, he was sure that the crime had been committed in that room and that only later was the body taken to Cristiana's room—by someone who'd had to force open the double doors of the bathroom by breaking the lock. And this "someone" could only be someone from the building, since they knew the layout and people's movements far too well.

When he returned to the bathroom, he heard his officer saying: "Wait here. The inspector will be back."

12

It was Cristiana's maid: powdered face, slim yet muscular body in a short dress with thin blue stripes, her blonde thatch topped with a lacy bonnet. She kept her hands in the pocket of her little white apron and seemed not the least perturbed.

"Are you Signora O'Brian's maid?"

"Verna Campbell."

A hard voice, which came from her head. She threw her name out as if in challenge and stared insolently at De Vincenzi.

"Did the *signora* bring you with her from America?"

"Yes."

So there were two of them: the other was Prospero O'Lary.

"Go out to the corridor." The officer joined his companion who'd already studied four of the herms and was now admiring the fifth.

"Sit down, Signorina Campbell."

The girl took a fresh look around before sitting down. She wouldn't glance over at the bed and De Vincenzi was sure that she either knew about or had guessed the presence of the body. He put on a show of good-natured friendliness.

"Is it tiring serving Signora O'Brian, Signorina Campbell?"

"If *doing nothing* is a fag, then service here is certainly tiring."

Following his habit of adopting the native language of those whose trust he wanted to gain, he spoke to Miss Campbell in English, and she used *far niente* in Italian for "doing nothing". But her tone remained cross, almost disengaged, with all her phrases rising at the end.

"Is that why you came with her from America to Italy?"

"I came with her because I need to earn money."

"Were you her maid over there too?"

"No. Mrs Sage hired me from the hotel where I was doing seasonal work in Miami. Since she offered to double my salary, I decided to come to Europe with her."

"Sage?"

"That was the lady's name, or at least the name of her husband."

"Is he dead?"

"I don't think so." A fleeting, sarcastic smile. Then the girl's eyes turned mocking.

Sage? De Vincenzi felt he'd heard the name before. Or rather, read. That was it: he must have read it in a book or some newspaper.

"Divorce?"

"If you like."

"What did Mr Sage do?"

"Robbed banks. He was renowned for it. It's just that no one knew him under his real name of Sage, except when he stood before the court in Rutland. Until then he was content to become famous under the name of Moran."

Edward Moran, sidekick of Machine-gun Kelly, Baby Face Nelson, John Dillinger… A phantom gangster, the one who'd hit up the Bank of Lincoln for a million dollars. But of course! De Vincenzi remembered him now perfectly, not because he was in the habit of following the exploits of American criminals, but because he'd come across quite an interesting book, *Persons in Hiding*, written by the head of the G-men, J. Edgar Hoover. He affected indifference.

"Nothing more natural than that the wife of such a villain should have wanted to divorce him and revert to her own name."

"Who said anything different? Are you sure O'Brian is her name?"

She pursed her lips in spite. Verna Campbell wasn't fond of her boss.

"So you came directly to Italy?"

"Yes. We disembarked in Naples, but after a few days there we went to Paris, and from Paris to London. Two months in London, and back to Paris again. We'd been in the French capital for three months and I thought we'd finally settled down there when the lady suddenly put us on a flight for Venice. We've only been in Milan for two years."

"That seems normal as well. Didn't it occur to you that Miss O'Brian was looking for the best place to establish her fashion house?" His smile was guileless. He'd discovered the woman's Achilles' heel and was trying to provoke her, make her speak. The ploy was successful.

"Oh, exactly! It was precisely because she wished to create a fashion house, one with lots of rich male clients for whom she'd do favours."

"Male clients? Are you sure you're not mistaken, Signorina Campbell? The rooms below are full of women."

She looked at him pityingly. She'd never met a policeman so indescribably obtuse, or even dreamt there could be one.

"Well, I could be mistaken."

Her condescending tone said: why bother obstructing this man when he's so trusting? But she looked at the telephone on the small table next to the bed and De Vincenzi followed her gaze. Beside the telephone was a small book in green leather.

"Do you want to take a look under here, Signorina Campbell?"

He got up and walked towards the bed. The girl watched him indifferently. He lifted up the edge of the bedspread to reveal the body.

Verna Campbell paled, but displayed neither fear nor uneasiness. Instead, the dull roar of anger, a fiery hatred.

"Did you know him?"

"I don't know him any more. At last he'll go to hell!"

De Vincenzi covered up the corpse once again. When it came down to it he was sentimental, and he had an instinctive respect for the dead, for scoundrels who'd once been alive. The girl's words, so icy and disrespectful, had upset him.

"Where were you today between two and four, Miss Campbell?" he asked in a hard voice.

"In my room."

"Where is your room?"

"On the second floor before you get to the atelier."

"Near the service stairs?"

"How did you know?"

"I don't know. I'm asking you."

"Exactly. But if you're thinking I might have killed… that man, you're making a big blunder. He's been avoiding me for some time."

"We'll come back to that, Signorina."

He accompanied her to the door. Verna Campbell left rapidly and disappeared down the service stairs. De Vincenzi let out a sigh. He was in a bad mood. The atmosphere was becoming increasingly charged and heavy with foreboding. He recognized his state of mind and it scared him, since it always heralded some catastrophe, as if the premonition itself had some power to act.

He returned to the bedside and looked at the small green book. He was almost afraid to touch it, but he overcame his repugnance, picked it up and leafed through it. It was an address book. The pages, divided alphabetically, contained only a few names and numbers. He read one or two of them, closed the book and put it in his pocket. It now seemed more important than ever for him to speak to the plump Evelina. A calm chat, a tête-à-tête, without interruptions, and above all, without heart attacks…

He ordered the two officers in the corridor: "Don't move from here. No one is to enter this room except the investigating magistrate."

13

At 6.30 p.m., Cristiana O'Brian's showrooms looked deserted. The catwalk show had been halted at 6 p.m.—before even half the designs had made their appearance: De Vincenzi had requested that Marta stop it before the scheduled time. He wouldn't disturb the ladies gathered there; it didn't seem necessary to question them. But he needed to have free rein. Besides, the investigating magistrate would be there before long and, right after that, the undertakers with the stretcher.

Marta and Clara had smilingly and obsequiously helped the clients to leave. Clara had put on a special smile and bow for the Boltons. As she walked them up to the door she said, "We trust that your sister will want to honour us with a few more visits, Mr Bolton."

"I'm sure she will, Signorina. My sister has always greatly admired your designs." John Bolton smiled again in the lift, this time smugly. Almost without moving his lips he said to Anna, "The game promises to be tricky. I saw her and spoke to her."

Anna Sage responded listlessly. "I don't see any use in your playing the same old game. Remember, in Miami you lost because you wanted to offer your relatives lunch on the Fourth of July."

"A memorable lunch, that was!"

And the most extraordinary visitor Federico had ever seen at the fashion house put another ten *lire* in his hand.

De Vincenzi was now free to move about in the empty show-rooms. He needed to order his thoughts, since he hadn't yet had time to take stock of the situation. He'd gathered many clues, but he couldn't connect them; they didn't add up to a complete picture. As he contemplated a collection of rhinestone and ormolu flower jewellery in a glass display case, he began to tot up the clues. The orchid was one of them, perhaps the most obscure of all, the one that might unexpectedly and accidentally reveal the solution. Right after that came the cold and unfathomable Verna Campbell, who'd made sure to give him disturbing information and enthralled him with tales of gangsters. The girl had done more than that: she'd revealed to him the importance of the green address book now in his pocket.

Evelina's sudden attack was another clue. Then there was the body's having been placed in Cristiana's bed… The list might still be incomplete.

Despite all this, no single, specific piece of information, no clue showed where the path began. Everything was murky and dark. Why had Cristiana O'Brian—who'd never been a dressmaker and didn't have any aptitude for it—felt it necessary to set up a fashion house? In and of itself, that fact certainly wouldn't have aroused anyone's surprise if Valerio hadn't been strangled. But both the crime and the crime scene cast a sinister light on the woman's activities. What's more, Valerio's murder didn't chime with all the rest. If it was a product of the environment, the staging seemed over-elaborate. *This wasn't the crime that was meant to happen. And De Vincenzi was startled to think what the real crime might be, and how it might have been carried out.*

The lights had been left on in the showrooms, and weak daylight was still filtering through the windows. The corridor looked deserted, but De Vincenzi heard the models chattering in their room even though Clara was there to keep an eye on them. Cristiana O'Brian was in the office with O'Lary, and Marta was with the dressmakers, whom De Vincenzi had prohibited from leaving their room.

So Evelina had to be in her office, waiting in trepidation for him to question her. He thought despairingly about the vast number of people he still had to interrogate. All the women would talk to him about Valerio. What could they tell him that would help to set him on the trail of the murderer? Nothing, probably. On the other hand, they might still reveal other facts about Valerio, and he'd be glad of that.

He took the medallion he'd found on the floor from his pocket. Had it actually belonged to Valerio? He'd been so sure it was his that he hadn't even bothered to check to see whether the dead man had had a chain it could have fallen off. He slowly went through the doorway of the third showroom, the last one on the same side as the internal lift. He was heading for the office when the models' voices, coming from behind the closed door, made him stop.

"You're being stupid to cry over him! He cared for you like he did the knot in his tie! He liked you, but as for loving you, he fooled you just like me and all the others."

"Be quiet, Irma! Don't you see that Gioia's hurting? It's a mood, and it'll pass. As it happens, he was in here a short time before he was killed, and he talked to her."

"I'll bet the American bumped him off... She couldn't accept it."

"What now? Have you seen the police everywhere? They're going to close this dump and send us packing."

"Oh, I couldn't care less! Fercioni have been after me for a while. I only have to go and see them for them to take me on."

De Vincenzi began walking down the corridor. Could this, then, be a crime of jealousy? Yes, it would have been possible to consider it one—if the body had not been taken to Cristiana's bed. But it's rare for a woman to have the strength for such gruesome work, even if she wants revenge against a rival. Could Cristiana have been in competition with her own maid, or with one of the models or dressmakers? It would all be very simple if things had gone like that. But they had not.

He went into Evelina's room. The door between Cristiana and Prospero's office was closed. De Vincenzi checked that first, and then looked at the bookkeeper's large desk. He noticed that the woman's head was bent over the ledger. Maybe Evelina had felt sleepy, or maybe she'd fallen over like that crying... Yet why should she be crying? How strange that he should consider that.

But then he saw something else that made his blood run cold. *On the corner of the desk was a glass, and in that glass was an orchid.*

De Vincenzi was at her side in a flash. He shook her, and her head rolled across the ledger but her body didn't move. He lifted her head: it fell back down. Yet he'd had time to see her face: Evelina was dead. The enormous woman was still warm, but she wasn't breathing. He tried to sit her up straight, to grab her wrists, but he realized immediately that it would be impossible to move her. All that flesh had become so heavy…

De Vincenzi felt lost for several moments. This new crime, committed practically under his nose, had shocked him and robbed him of any initiative, his power to analyse or to act. From the moment he'd set foot in this building, it had all been happening around him. It was bewildering.

He moved away from the body and walked around the room randomly. It was surprising that he'd managed not to scream, not to call anyone and, above all, not to run. Even a police inspector is a man. He felt like someone had slapped him. He'd been at this job for twenty years without managing to get a grip on his emotions. A body is a body, and that's that. So why should this one upset him more than any other?

He went over to the window, drew back the silk curtain, put his forehead against the glass and stayed like that for a few minutes. He called on his reason, and succeeded in discovering why he'd had such a shock. Nothing had given a greater impression of life—intense, physical, overflowing—than Evelina's body when he'd seen it in motion, *alive*. That body was now motionless, heavy, a mass as enormous as it was inert, and the violent contrast gave her death a frightening meaning, rendering it material, visible. That, rather than anything else, had to be the reason for his fleeting feeling of loss.

Calmer now, he went back to the body and studied it. From her neck, it was clear that she'd been strangled. Yet Evelina's killer had not used his hands. The marks covered her neck: wide, deep and black. A curious chain of bruises. The woman had been strangled with a necklace.

He finally succeeded in righting the body so that it stayed against the back of the chair. Hanging against Evelina's breast he noticed a glass necklace whose shiny black beads were held together by a thick silk thread. He tested its strength and was convinced that the pull of a finger alone wouldn't have broken it. Without a doubt, the necklace was the murder weapon.

He let Evelina's torso fall once more against the table, settled her dangling head on the ledger and walked over to the door of the offices, opening it suddenly.

Standing next to the rosewood table, Prospero O'Lary was talking to Cristiana, who listened to him as she smoked. Madame Firmino was still sitting in the chair he'd found her in, and appeared to be absorbed in contemplation of the smoke spiralling up from her cigarette. Prospero O'Lary was saying, "I told you, Cristiana, I don't know the symbolism of the orchid. I only know the meaning of the aster."

14

"Have any of you been out of this room?"

De Vincenzi marvelled at the harsh, cutting tone of his own voice. It was coming from somewhere outside him, and it made him stiffen. His face was tense.

Madame Firmino leapt to her feet, no longer the least bit listless. Prospero O'Lary twitched too, and went white in the face. Cristiana simply turned towards De Vincenzi, exhibiting no sign of surprise.

"I certainly haven't!" Dolores suddenly realized that the man standing in the door wasn't the same one she'd spoken with earlier. "Has something else happened?" she added anxiously.

Cristiana looked at Dolores, then at Prospero. She asked in a voice that was unchanged: raspy, bitter and unpleasant, "Have you found Valerio's killer?"

De Vincenzi left her question hanging and went straight for Prospero. He took him by the lapels of his frock coat and shook him.

"Answer me! How long have you been in this room?"

"Well, I don't know. Since I came down. You actually saw me come in, and then shortly afterwards she joined me." He pointed to Cristiana and freed himself from De Vincenzi's grip, smoothing his lapels in an effort to straighten them.

"Did you hear anything coming from the next room?"

"Not a sound. We didn't even hear you open the door. We were talking, and you must admit that we have the right to be so absorbed in our jobs that we don't notice what's going on outside here."

"So not one of you three can tell me who killed Signorina Evelina?"

Prospero's face went bright red. "What did you say?" His every emotion lit up his head like an electric signal.

The two women stared at De Vincenzi incredulously. It seemed that neither of them could take in the meaning of the words they'd heard.

Cristiana got up and stubbed out her cigarette in the bottom of a crystal bowl.

"I don't believe Evelina can be involved in this matter, Inspector."

"As it happens, now that someone's killed her, she won't have anything more to do with it." He paused, staring at the three faces, one after the other, with such intensity that it was distressing for him too. As he watched them, he saw the two women finally take in the horrifying news. They were overcome with fear—animal fear, pure and simple. As for Prospero, his own eyes were brimming with terror as he sought to avoid De Vincenzi's gaze.

"That's all for the moment. Ladies, you'll stay here. Follow me, Signor O'Lary."

He walked over to the door, opened it and let O'Lary go out first. He then closed the door behind them. The little man took several steps towards the desk and stopped. He looked at the body. His ruddy, apoplectic colour had disappeared. He adjusted his glasses on his nose, took another step. And, as if finally sure that he was seeing things correctly, he suddenly looked desolate and shook his head slowly and incessantly. It stood out a bit from his collar, and at the sight of that shiny, bare head bobbing away rhythmically, De Vincenzi formed a clear image of a black tortoise ill with meningitis.

"Do you have anything to say, Signor O'Lary?"

"I'd say we need to find the murderer immediately. We're all in danger of being strangled!"

Prospero O'Lary's fear might have seemed comical, not to say hilarious, if De Vincenzi hadn't been standing in front of Evelina's dead body.

"Oh, I don't think we all are."

"What do you mean? Don't you see that these are the crimes of a crazy maniac? Such crimes occur only in Europe!" Prospero began shaking his head as if overcome by an epileptic fit.

"Is that what you think? It's one theory. But perhaps you'd tell me how you knew that Evelina had been strangled?"

The head instantly stopped its bobbing. Prospero's eyelids fluttered.

"What?"

"Is it clear, looking at that body, that she was strangled to death?"

"Of course it's clear!"

And "Oremus" pointed to Evelina's neck. Her head was lying with one ear on the ledger and indeed, one could see the other side of her face and neck and the blackish marks left by her necklace. There was no opportunity for De Vincenzi to gain a point, but he had regained his lucidity and his capacity for detachment, which allowed him to observe others as well as himself as if the action and the tragedy were taking place on another plane or an imaginary stage.

"We'll speak shortly, Signor O'Lary. I need to give some orders first."

He went out to the corridor and called his two officers. He put one of them on guard in the corridor; the other he ordered to phone San Fedele to inform them about the new crime and to have the deputy inspector, Sani, come to Corso del Littorio with more officers from the flying squad.

"Phone for a doctor as well, then come back here at once. And tell Sani to bring a photographer."

After he'd given his orders he was struck by the feeling he always had in these cases: it was his absolute duty to set the official machine of justice in motion—with all its rules and procedures, red tape and useful scientific techniques. Yet he couldn't help but think how powerless that machine was to unveil the perpetrator of the crimes, given that the killer had to be present, visible and recognizable, and only someone who knew how to read the murderer's soul could unmask them. The person who'd murdered Valerio and Evelina was not a maniac as Prospero O'Lary believed and wanted everyone else to believe. Of that De Vincenzi was sure.

"Signor O'Lary, find a sheet, some fabric, a cover. We can't leave her poor, lifeless body as a spectacle."

O'Lary hurried into the corridor and De Vincenzi locked the door after him. Now he needed a few minutes to look round without any bystanders. He made sure that the door into the office was locked before quickly walking back to the desk. He looked at the body and the surface of the table. Evelina had been making her entries when she'd been killed. Given the position of the body and the expression on the dead woman's face—which seemed normal, calm, even if naturally a bit flushed—it was clear and indisputable that she must have known her killer well enough for them not to have aroused her suspicion. *Someone had been able to speak to her, approach her, slip behind her and then suddenly grab her necklace, squeezing it against her throat until she was dead.* De Vincenzi noticed the position of the chair Evelina had been sitting on. It leant back against the wall, as the desk was parallel to the line of the windows and actually sat in the space between two of them. How had the killer got behind the chair without Evelina's having expressly given them permission, and why in the world would she have allowed it? It was a question without an answer—until the sight of the telephone cleared up the mystery.

Here, as in Cristiana's office, the telephone was placed on a small table beside the chair and slightly behind it, next to the wall. The explanation was obvious: the killer had pretended to make a call—or had actually telephoned. Then, taking advantage of the momentary lapse in Evelina's attention, perhaps while she was focused on her accounts, they had acted quickly and expertly. This theory—the only plausible one—confirmed the other: it had been someone familiar enough to have the right to telephone without alarming Evelina or making her want to prevent them. Yes, it was all clear, but at the same time troubling.

If the number of suspects was beginning to shrink, it was becoming more difficult to distinguish the killer amongst them, or at least to find the motive for the crime. *Why had Evelina been murdered?* De Vincenzi couldn't see anything on the desk that would constitute an interesting clue. Nothing besides the usual things. Without touching the body, he quickly opened the side drawers: paper, bills, accounts. Some chequebooks and paying-in books from two city banks—in Cristiana O'Brian's name, of course. In the bottom right drawer he found a black leather purse that must have belonged to Evelina. He opened it. A handkerchief, a mirror, a wallet, a small bunch of keys, a phial of smelling salts, a comb, a tram pass in the name of Evelina Rossi and two opened letters addressed to her. He just had time to notice that they were both from Milan when someone began knocking insistently at the door after trying the handle. He put the two letters in his pocket, shut the purse and the drawer and went over to open the door.

"Come in, Signor O'Lary. I must have been distracted and turned the key in the lock automatically."

"Oremus" held out a large sheet. De Vincenzi covered the body with it. "That's done then, Signor O'Lary."

The white shroud gave the desk and Evelina's enormous body the appearance of a strange monument about to be unveiled. The orchid remained on the corner outside the sheet, adding to the scene's grotesque effect.

"What a nightmare, Inspector!"

"It certainly is. But you can sit down, O'Lary. Didn't I say we'd have to have a chat?" He put the glass down. At last he said quietly, "Signor O'Lary, why don't you talk to me a bit about Sage—or, if you prefer, Edward Moran? Since you're from America, you surely must know something about him."

This time the little man's glasses fell off. He didn't catch them in time, and the lenses splintered on the floor.

15

"So you say your husband was here today?"

"Yes."

For the twenty minutes Cristiana O'Brian had been with De Vincenzi she had uttered nothing but monosyllables. He felt as if he were interrogating a three-legged table at a séance: one knock for "yes", two for "no", and he knew full well that ninety-nine per cent of her answers were made up, as if for the table.

Getting O'Lary to speak had been easier. As soon as the little man was attacked head on, he deflated. He tried several times to deny it, but ultimately he confirmed the information given by Verna Campbell, albeit reluctantly. Russell Sage, better known as Edward Moran, was to all intents and purposes the head of a criminal gang. He'd committed so many crimes that no one could ever put an exact number to them when he was finally arrested. Russell had actually had a double life. Under the name of Sage, he appeared to be an honest businessman, and so he was: a perfectly normal rep for a manufacturing firm. He stayed in large hotels, visited famous seaside resorts and after he married lived in sumptuous apartments, taking his young wife to all the society gatherings.

Of course, under the name of Edward Moran the man was quite something else. Even Dillinger had admired him, recognizing his genius in planning and executing bank robberies. It was rare for a hold-up he'd organized to fail—if ever. He never worked twice with the same gang: within the group he was the star, signed up for one job and that was it. But he got a king's ransom every time. That said, no one had ever heard of Moran's having used his weapons for any purpose other than intimidation. He had no bodies on his conscience, or at least none that could be personally ascribed to him. Of course he had his men, the ones he'd order to get rid of traitors, spies, anyone who lacked the common sense to understand how dangerous he was, how much they ought to fear him, how reckless, how foolish it could be to blackmail him. But he had no blood on his hands, and was proud of his girlish squeamishness around the wounded. So when the Feds finally succeeded in apprehending him, the court of Rutland could do nothing apart from condemn him to a maximum of seven years in Alcatraz, where his companions—from Al Capone to Harvey Bailey—were already waiting for him.

"When?" De Vincenzi had asked.

"In 1936," O'Lary replied.

"But it hasn't been seven years yet?"

"He'll have been pardoned. He knew how to be the perfect gentleman—that is, when he wasn't robbing banks!"

When they got to the subject of Cristiana, Prospero O'Lary's loquacity came to a sudden halt. Yes, Cristiana had married Russell Sage; yes, she was *perhaps* ignorant of his true identity; yes, the woman had fled from him, abandoning him in Portland when the G-men were closing in on him. But the little man knew nothing else for certain—or he didn't want to say any more. How had he met Cristiana? He'd met her in Miami and had agreed to leave with her. The woman had confided in him on the high seas, when their ship the *Rex* was already headed for Europe. These were the fruits of the interview with Prospero O'Lary.

The doctor and magistrate had then shown up, and the photographer, along with Sani and the other officers from the flying squad. De Vincenzi had put someone on guard on all three floors of the fashion house and had all the rooms searched apart from the office, where Cristiana O'Brian and Madame Firmino had remained undisturbed. He'd attended the questioning of the dressmakers and the models. The two bodies were taken to the mortuary. And so evening had arrived, followed by night.

It was ten o'clock now and Madame Firmino had left, saying she was going to bed. De Vincenzi had sat across from Cristiana in her office and begun the interview which had taken on such a laconic form on her side. He'd gleaned from O'Lary the fact that Russell Sage had made an appearance in the fashion house that very day, though O'Lary had hurried to state that it had to be pure coincidence, since he didn't believe that Cristiana's husband would have committed those two crimes. What's more, O'Lary said that Cristiana had told him of Russell's presence, and that she'd spoken to her husband in her own room while De Vincenzi was questioning Madame Firmino on the first floor. Having established this, it had been easy for De Vincenzi to learn during his questioning with Marta, Clara, Federico and Rosetta that John Bolton and his sister had attended the catwalk show and to identify in the ruddy, good-natured American the legendary and fearsome outlaw.

"So you have no idea how John Bolton discovered where your room was and how to get to it?"

"No."

"Not even who might have sent him the invitation?"

"No."

Cristiana exhibited no sign of abnormality apart from her persistent monosyllabic answers.

"Listen to me, Signora. What has happened in this house over the last ten hours isn't only tragic, it's frightening, grotesque and absurd."

Cristiana bowed her head in agreement.

"Of course, these two crimes will be explained sooner or later, and then even their absurdity will seem logical. But at the moment I'd like to draw your attention to something, and I'd ask you not to make things more difficult for me by remaining mute."

A faint smile crossed her face. "But I *am* answering your questions, Inspector! It's not my fault if they only require a yes or a no."

"Fine. That something is this. Why was there an orchid in your room, and why was there another on Evelina's table? Does the flower have some special meaning for you?"

"My husband loves flowers. He often brought me an orchid when he came back home."

"It's quite a stretch to suppose that your husband could have committed the first crime, since I don't see how he could have killed Valerio, carried his body to your bed and left the building, only to re-enter it at around four-thirty, that is, when the body was discovered. Even allowing for all those exceptional talents that made him famous in America, I refuse to believe he performs miracles, and I refuse absolutely to believe that he masterminded Evelina's murder, which was committed while the showrooms were empty and after he and his sister had left. Coming in unseen would have been completely impossible at that time because all the entrances were being guarded by my men. Therefore, Signora, if the orchids weren't brought into your house by Russell Sage—and I don't see why he'd have done so, since he wanted to talk to you and he wouldn't have had any need to resort to flowers to revive your memory of him—who did bring them here, and why?"

"If I could solve puzzles like that so quickly, Inspector, do you think I'd be stuck here with you, worrying over those two bodies? My exceptional gifts of divination would have allowed me to foresee and prevent the murders. You're the one who'll have to answer the *Who?* and *Why?*"

"You're right, Signora. The duty falls to me, unfortunately." And De Vincenzi stood up.

"I won't solve them tonight, though, even if the absurdity of the situation, which the murderer purposely devised, might help me. I do however advise you, Signora, to take refuge in your room, or any other room you like. The house is under surveillance inside and out. I don't think there will be any other unfortunate events—at least until tomorrow."

"And you'll be back tomorrow?"

"I'll be back, Signora."

"And you'll explain the mystery?"

"I'll try to explain it."

"Goodnight, Inspector."

"Good luck, Signora O'Brian. But you haven't told me where you mean to spend the night."

"Where? Oh God—even though I fainted today, which must make me seem over-sensitive, I don't believe I have to give up my bed just because a cadaver was lying on it earlier. Nor do I see where else I'd sleep. There aren't any guest rooms in this building, not even enough comfortable sofas."

She too got to her feet and headed for the door. De Vincenzi followed and watched her as she went through Evelina's room and down the corridor as far as the lift. She turned round.

"Goodnight, Inspector."

A few seconds later she'd disappeared. For once, he did what he said he would do and left Cristiana O'Brian's building. Outside, no doubt, the mystery wouldn't seem so baffling.

DAY TWO:
FRIDAY

1

The first day of March was rainy, windy and, where the dust had turned to slush in the outlying streets, muddy too.

In the apartment he'd rented on via Massena near Sempione Park, De Vincenzi got up from his bed at seven, perfectly rested if not completely calm. The crimes at the O'Brian Fashion House had been tormenting him when he'd got home at midnight, but he'd immersed himself in a book by Anatole France in an effort to forget them. He adored those now-forgotten books, and fell asleep quickly. Once awake, however, the two dead bodies immediately reappeared, and that grim memory, the sight of the leaden sky and the drizzle splattering the window put paid to any calm he'd felt. On principle he hadn't wanted to analyse the two crimes during the night or to revisit the various troubling points they presented. Since he believed in the value of psychological clues alone, he would trust his intuition. His colleagues wryly called him a poet, and when it came down to it they weren't mistaken, even though they didn't consider it praise.

As he soaked in the bathtub, he thought about his confounded need to dig deep into people's souls, and since his own spirits were low he sneered at himself. Nothing but a poor old fool. All that psychology, and someone had killed poor Evelina practically under his nose. She certainly didn't deserve such a miserable end. She undoubtedly held at least one of the keys to the mystery, keys he'd now have to find in goodness knows what dark hole.

He was getting dressed and at the same time sipping the coffee brought to him by the maternal Antonietta when he remembered the two letters he'd found in the dead woman's purse. He'd put them in his pocket and forgotten they were there. One of them was from a mobile library to which Evelina belonged, asking her to return a book she'd borrowed two months before. The letter was polite but expressed surprise that a reader as quick and passionate as Signorina Rossi could have kept a book for so long. The volume in question was a romance novel by Mura. De Vincenzi put the letter back in the envelope. Not a ray of light—but perhaps just a flicker: in the last two months Evelina had had such a lot of work or so many worries that she couldn't concentrate on reading, which must have been the dreamy old spinster's favourite diversion.

The second letter at first seemed more promising, even if he wasn't aware at the time of its real importance. It was typewritten on paper without any letterhead, and following the address and the date were these words:

> *Our brief telephone conversation, Signorina, was not sufficient. I believe you may be helpful to me if, as you stated, you really wish to be. I'll expect you, therefore, tomorrow evening at 21.00 in my private office on via Catalani 75, near Loreto. You will be handsomely rewarded for the trouble you've taken and which you have yet to undertake for me.*
>
> *Yours faithfully*

No signature. It was dated the 8th of March. Evelina, therefore, was set to go to the appointment on the very day she died. Had someone killed her to prevent her going? There was nothing to support that theory, but De Vincenzi told himself that it was crucial to trace the unknown correspondent, even if turned out to be a pointless waste of time.

Crucial and essential—even more so than meeting the Boltons, which he'd promised himself he'd do that morning. The two siblings—who were staying in the Albergo Palazzo, as he'd learnt from Anna Bolton's invitation, which Clara had kept back—could wait. As far as De Vincenzi was concerned it wasn't Russell Sage, now John Bolton, who'd killed Valerio and Evelina, even if the whole mystery appeared to revolve around him, as the two orchids seemed to suggest. De Vincenzi didn't believe the outlaw was guilty—not even of the theatrical and symbolic presence of the flowers beside the bodies.

He phoned Sani at San Fedele, who reassured him that nothing had disturbed the tranquillity of the O'Brian Fashion House during the night. Sani had left there at seven in the morning, while everyone was still sleeping; Cruni remained with the other officers.

"Go and get some rest for a few hours. You'll be needing it. I'll take care of Corso del Littorio. Come back to the office this afternoon." He was fond of his deputy, and his words resonated with affectionate concern.

He chose a roundabout route and, after taking two trams, one more crowded than the other, De Vincenzi arrived in via Catalani at nine o'clock. Splashing through the mud and rain he found 75, a small house without any number or other signage at the entrance. He didn't bother inventing a pretext for his appearance at the home of Evelina's unknown correspondent and, trusting to the inspiration of the moment, pressed the bell.

The door was opened by a haughty and disdainful elderly woman wearing a white apron over her black dress. By spinning her a story about how he was looking for a small house to let, he managed to discover that this one belonged to a *commendatore* who found it convenient for the occasional break, but only ever stayed for a few hours. With persistence, and displaying his police badge to the shocked woman, De Vincenzi learnt the name of the owner, a fairly well-known banker, possibly a millionaire.

He found himself back in the mud, in the middle of the road, with a set of directions. Even if they proved to be important, this would be a tough nut to crack. And yet postponing his visit wouldn't ensure him a better welcome, so it seemed more urgent than ever that he go.

This time he took a taxi to Piazza della Scala. Although the huge waiting room at the internationally renowned banking institute was chock full of people, the *commendatore* received him without delay. He was a stout man, rough-hewn, all lined and wrinkled, with the watery pallor of a diabetic. De Vincenzi realized immediately that his title of police inspector was the open sesame, and that the *commendatore* was worried. More than worried. Afraid.

He gestured for De Vincenzi to sit and sat looking at him.

"I've asked you to come in straight away, despite my being extremely busy. But I don't understand."

"Of course." Polite both by nature and habit, De Vincenzi now appeared disarmingly smooth. "How could you understand?

But perhaps this letter will help." He held out the letter he'd found in Evelina's purse.

The *commendatore* recognized it without reading it, and he became even more agitated.

"How ever did this letter fall into the hands of the police?"

"For tragic reasons: the woman to whom it was addressed has been murdered."

The man started. He seemed momentarily lost, but quickly regained his composure. The colour returned to his cheeks, his eyes grew steely and his face tensed. He shifted things around on his desk as if re-establishing order in front of him. But the reorganization and calculation were actually taking place internally.

"You realize, Inspector, that this business must be conducted with a great deal of tact and delicacy?"

"Oh, I assure you I know that all too well!" De Vincenzi sighed.

"How did you find out that the letter was from me?"

"There's an address on it."

"And old Sofia told you."

"Old? Not very. But yes, old Sofia had to tell me, Commendatore."

"I see." He pushed at a large crystal ball, picked up a pen and replaced it. "What do you want from me?"

"I want you to help me understand. Nothing else. Think it over. What I'm asking is completely risk-free for you. My only goal in coming here is to find a lead that will take me to the murderer."

The *commendatore* peered at De Vincenzi, trying to read him. He made his deductions quickly and decided on a certain *froideur*, which he adopted in money matters and which had brought him his wealth.

"Where do I come into it?"

"You can easily help me to understand why someone would kill a calm, peaceful woman weighing more than a hundred kilos and suffering from heart attacks. We always need a motive."

"What do you want to know, then?"

A humble, bashful smile preceded De Vincenzi's reply. "Everything, Commendatore. Everything."

"The woman approached me by phone."

"When?"

"About a week ago."

"And she wanted…"

"Yes, I'll tell you. But I ask for your discretion, your absolute silence. May I count on that?"

"I believe so. What I mean is, I think I understand what you're about to tell me and that, therefore, I can see to it that your name is kept out of the inquest."

"What do you think I'm about to tell you?"

His method: getting others to speak in order to gain the upper hand.

De Vincenzi smiled. "I've seen your secret villa, Commendatore, and I know Madama Cristiana O'Brian and her fashion house."

"So you've gathered that Cristiana was blackmailing me!" he exploded. "Yes. She's been doing it for a year now. I took a friend to her fashion house and I was a damned idiot to pay her bills personally. After the second bill was paid, that woman—O'Brian—telephoned me to say that she knew my private address, my family's address, and she was afraid that one of her bumbling employees had sent a copy of the bill to my wife by mistake. Clever, no?"

"Rather."

"I paid. And naturally I forbade my friend to set foot again in that filthy den of blackmailers. Would you believe it?"

"Yes, I believe it, Commendatore."

"After a month, another telephone call. O'Brian told me she'd noticed that my friend had stopped coming to her. She said, regretfully, that the same bumbling employee was about to write to my private address to suggest other designs that would certainly appeal to the taste of the person I was protecting. What could I do? I paid again."

De Vincenzi rose. "Thank you, Commendatore, and please excuse the disturbance."

"Don't you want to know anything else?"

"The rest I can imagine. Signorina Evelina discovered her boss's plot and phoned you in turn, offering to stop it."

"Exactly. Another blackmail."

"But no! I think not. That poor thing would have been on the level. She believed she could stop Cristiana O'Brian's criminal activity—and maybe she really could. It may be that she'd discovered another secret she could use with Cristiana, one that would render her powerless with you and the others. Because, of course, you wouldn't have been the only one to have fallen into that typically American-style trap."

"On the level!" exclaimed the *commendatore*, genuinely amazed.

"Otherwise, why would she have been murdered? Yes, I understand: to eliminate a rival. But I assume she approached you in good faith. You can't weigh more than a hundred kilos without having a correspondingly light conscience!"

When he got to the door, something occurred to De Vincenzi. He turned and went back to the desk. "Excuse me. One last question. Was it a young man with dark hair, quite good-looking, who came to get the money for O'Brian?"

"Shameless! Yes, that's him."

"I see. Well, it'll console you to know that that young man has also been murdered."

In the lift, De Vincenzi stood watching a young man in brown put a finger in the collar of his constricting uniform. He took Cristiana O'Brian's small green address book from his jacket pocket and at N he found the name of the *commendatore* from whom he'd just taken his leave.

2

The day had begun well for De Vincenzi even though it was still raining. He'd come up with a convincing reason for the murders of Evelina and Valerio: Evelina might have been killed because she'd got involved in Cristiana's unsavoury dealings and Valerio because he was becoming awkward. This would mean that Cristiana O'Brian was responsible for a double murder. Who else would have had a motive for making a difficult, even dangerous, assistant disappear, or for ensuring that Evelina kept quiet for ever?

However, though Cristiana had a typical liar's personality, and one might be able to credit her with the requisite criminal know-how gleaned from living in that environment in America, one couldn't forget that Valerio's body had been found on her bed, *and this was something she'd never have done.* De Vincenzi realized that she'd never have carried Valerio's body to her own bed after killing him in the "museum of horrors". Besides, there was the "coincidence" of John Bolton's sudden arrival and the deliberately symbolic appearance of the orchids.

It was already eleven by the time De Vincenzi got off the tram in Piazzale Fiume.

John Bolton and his sister Anna occupied an extremely luxurious apartment on the second floor of the Albergo Palazzo, where they received De Vincenzi straight away. The man who'd been the king of American bank robbers and now wanted to appear as the peaceable John Bolton was waiting for De

Vincenzi in the sitting room. He stood next to a table where a few antique coins, greenish-yellow and corroded, lay next to a volume bound in red leather. He was smiling and wearing his gold-rimmed spectacles.

"I've been offered these coins, but I've only found one that's worth anything. They'd have me believe it's one of the coins with a Kufic legend struck in the Kingdom of Naples and Sicily, and they brought this book to show me. It's from the series on these coins published in 1844 by Domenico Spinelli, Prince of San Giorgio. I'm dubious about the coin's authenticity, but I'll end up taking it, with the proviso that I can show it to Alföldi on my next trip to Vienna."

He spoke without affectation, his accent strangely pitched between irony and teasing. While he listened, De Vincenzi took a look round. The room was full of flowers, in pots and vases. They were everywhere—on tables, the console, the floor in front of the window—but not an orchid amongst them.

Bolton approached De Vincenzi.

"To what do I owe your visit, Signor Detective?"

"I see you're passionate about flowers," he said with a smile, "and I've come straight from a house where I saw two orchids yesterday, one next to each of the bodies…"

Bolton furrowed his brow and took off his glasses. He was clearly unaccustomed to looking through them and wanted to watch his adversary carefully.

"What sort of conversation is this? Why are you talking to me about bodies?"

"Because there are some, and because you saw at least one of them, Signor… Bolton."

"Oh, so that's it! Cristiana told you all about me." He shrugged with indifference and indicated the sofa. "Would you like to sit down so I can provide some explanation?"

He sat and waited for De Vincenzi to join him.

"So, my dear Ileana told you everything."

"Actually, she didn't. Or rather, she wasn't the first to tell me."

"I don't understand."

It seemed to De Vincenzi that having someone else in on his secret was upsetting Bolton, and he instinctively made up his mind not to mention Prospero O'Lary. "It's not important, really. I suspect that when you came here to find your wife, you were prepared for the possibility that you might be recognized. And I suppose that, apart from a certain sort of publicity, you knew you wouldn't meet any real danger if it became known that you are Russell Sage, sentenced to seven years by the court of Rutland—"

"—and let off for good conduct, as it happens."

"And you emigrated to Europe because?..."

"Change of air, Signor Detective! What do you think? When you decide to turn over a new leaf, you need to live in another climate, circulate in another environment with a different set of people who don't know you any more than you know them."

"Turn over a new leaf?"

"Completely." He spoke with great seriousness and came across as utterly sincere. "Ah, yes, my friend. I'm not making myself out to be better than I am. But I'm getting older, and certain—how shall I put it?—certain activities require youthful vigour, impetuosity, faith in yourself. After my spell in Alcatraz, I felt a bit rusty. Tired, and unable to go back to my double life again. I had to choose between one of my two lives, and either surrender completely to criminal life—as you can see, these aren't words that frighten me—or settle down as a businessman, maybe in manufacturing, and by doing so completely satisfy my interest in books, coins, rare and beautiful things. I preferred the second alternative since it seemed more relaxing. I'm getting older, I tell you! Which means the change had to be radical. I rounded up what was left and departed for Europe with my sister."

"And you immediately started looking for your wife."

"Not right away, and not on purpose."

"Here, you found yourself confronted with a body and an orchid. Were you aware that there are now two bodies?"

It was the orchid that really struck Bolton, since he exclaimed, "An orchid? It's the second time you've mentioned it." He was genuinely surprised.

"Aren't you a flower lover?" De Vincenzi glanced at the roses, zinnias, violas, irises and gladioli in turn.

"Ah, so that's it?" Bolton's face hardened; his brain was turning over. There was a brief silence. "Let's speak frankly, Signor Detective. I deal with situations; I always have. This is why I knew the federal laws over there better than a judge. Your laws aren't as familiar to me, but I have some experience of men. So: you suspect I'm behind that murder. I don't believe you want to charge me with the other body we've spoken about, right? You're here to make me talk and then you'll say, 'Russell, my friend, anything you say from now on can and will be used against you.'"

De Vincenzi laughed. "Oh, but in Italy we're not obliged to caution criminals like that when we arrest them!"

"So are you arresting me?"

"It's precisely what I'm *not* doing, Signor Sage. I have no proof that you strangled Valerio."

Russell Sage looked at his hands and asked, "Did you say Valerio? I don't know him."

"Maybe. But you do know the O'Brian Fashion House well enough to be able to find your wife's room without anyone escorting you there or seeing you. It must have been the first time you'd set foot in the business on Corso del Littorio."

"Well, it was the first time, Signor Detective." He rose. "May I?" He disappeared through the door that led from the sitting room to the other rooms in the suite. He returned in a moment with two envelopes. "Look at these, Signor Detective."

One was the blue envelope of the O'Brian Fashion House, showing its pierced dove logo, with the typewritten address of Mr John Bolton, Albergo Palazzo. The other, white envelope was larger and contained a sheet that had been folded in four to make it fit. De Vincenzi opened it.

It was a plan, a detailed plan of the first and third floors of the fashion house, with arrows indicating the route—via the service stairs—to Cristiana's room. But the little rectangle was captioned: *Ileana Sage's bedroom*. De Vincenzi looked over at Russell, who nodded.

"That's how I learnt where my wife was and what name she was hiding behind—from these two letters which arrived the other day: that is, the day before the event. I'd come to Italy intending to look her up, because I knew she was here. I knew that because I'd followed her to Paris, and she escaped me just when I discovered through a private detective agency where she lived. I was about to go and see her. But if it hadn't been for these two letters, I wouldn't have discovered so soon that Cristiana O'Brian was Ileana. Who sent them to me, and why? Those were the very questions I was asking myself before you arrived, Signor Detective. I began asking them the moment I found Ileana beside a body. I decided it was both pressing and wise to get out of there as quickly as possible."

"And now?"

Russell put his gold-rimmed spectacles back on and looked at De Vincenzi, smiling good-naturedly.

"I now think someone was trying to trap me by showing me the way to Ileana's room—*because there was a body in there.* Add the orchid to all this in order to finger me, since I love flowers, and you have the picture."

He appeared perfectly confident now, and De Vincenzi asked himself if he really suspected Cristiana. But for the time being, Russell Sage, refashioned as John Bolton, must have told De Vincenzi everything he could—unless he was keeping him sweet with a stack of lies, one after the other, each appearing to be the truth.

He put the two envelopes in his pocket. Bolton watched him as he did so, once more smiling affably.

"We may see each other again, Signor Bolton."

"It would give me great pleasure, Signor Detective. I plan to stay in Milan for quite some time." He escorted De Vincenzi to the lift.

"Would you like to see your wife again?" De Vincenzi asked as he got into the lift.

"I believe it will be necessary, Signor Detective."

3

The girls turned towards the door as it opened. Irma was doing her nails with a towel spread over her knees and Anna was reading a flyer about a romantic film, *A Dream of Love*. Gioia sat motionless, hands on her knees, chin squared. The only thing that made her interesting was her blue eyes, clearly defined by long lashes, and the youthful freshness of her skin. She was staring straight ahead with such a dark look on her face that it seemed as if she were about to cry.

Clara appeared in the doorway and glanced at the card in her hands. "Hurry up, girls! There's a crowd. Anna, put on 2412; Irma, 2437. And Gioia, you get into 75 from the evening gowns with capes," she ordered. She turned and yelled into the corridor, "Papina, come and help the models!" She repeated the three numbers after checking them on her card and then disappeared. Irma threw the towel and her nail file in the air.

"I told you so. Eleven-thirty, and it's starting already. This whole day is going to be a laugh, just wait and see! And after yesterday's crimes, the clients will be coming in droves to see the designs, just to snoop. It stinks of corpses in here!" She opened the wardrobe and slid through the numbers. "I knew it. Number 2437 is the one I hate!"

She took the hanger and removed the garment, throwing it on the carpet. Quickly wriggling out of her skirt, she tugged at her jacket zipper and she too appeared in her white silk chemise, tall and imposing as a young willow.

"Quick, Papina. Get the trousers ready for me. It's just the right day for beachwear!"

Papina had grey hair and a purple face. She was like a trained mouse, one of those small white ones that sit up on their tails and then fall flat, their stomachs slapping the ground. She got up on her tail and stayed there through some miracle of balance, to the confusion of all who saw her walking around on her little bow legs and funny round feet. Yet her hands were so quick and lively that one couldn't even feel her buttoning up a dress, lacing a belt or pulling a skirt round the hips to adjust it.

As she took the blue trousers and yellow sash from the wardrobe for Irma, she walked behind Gioia and shook the girl's shoulders.

"Quickly, my lovely! If you sit there under a spell, the prince can't carry you off to the *wedding*..."

She'd read all the fairy stories and took delight in being irresistibly droll, so instead of *wedding* she'd said *werewolf*; she was imitating Macario, whom she'd seen at the cinema.

Gioia stood up, shook herself and started taking off the black dress she was wearing. Anna went over to her.

"Be brave, darling! You've had a tooth pulled, and in a short while you won't feel any more pain. What can you do? It's probably better this way."

Gioia looked at her like a frustrated dog and sighed.

"You say that because you didn't know him like I did. We were going to be married."

"Him?!" Irma burst into laughter as she put on her trousers.

But Anna gave her such a hard shove that she had to lean against the wardrobe in order not to fall over.

"Can't you see she's really suffering?"

"She's a fool to suffer. Valerio wasn't worth it."

"Well shut up, then!"

Gioia's eyes were full of tears.

"Come on, lovely! Now you'll need your make-up artist. Sit here while I tell you a *yoke*…" And Papina, armed with a handkerchief, wiped her tears dry with one hand while helping her to take off her dress with the other.

Just then, De Vincenzi appeared in the corridor, coming from the direction of the lift. He'd arrived at Corso del Littorio a few minutes before and no one had seen him yet apart from Cruni and the doorman. He stopped by the open door of the models' room and looked in. Anna saw him and said, "Yeeees…" The other girls turned round and fell silent.

He smiled. "Good morning, ladies. I'm here to speak to you as well."

Marta's voice came from behind him.

"Good morning, Inspector. They're waiting for the girls in the showroom. Couldn't you question them later?"

"But of course! What are you doing? Is it another catwalk show?"

"Oh, no. But the clients are here. They've asked to see a few dresses and we always show them on the girls."

"I see."

He started for the door of the office, stealing a glance at Marta beside him.

"You're busy too?"

"No, Clara will take care of it. And anyway, I doubt it will come to anything. Those ladies are here because of the scandal. Have you read the papers?"

De Vincenzi smiled. "It was inevitable. What about Signora O'Brian?"

"She's in her room. I haven't seen her yet this morning. I think she's suffering."

"That's also inevitable. May I go in?" He put a hand to the door—the one through which Evelina must have passed so many times.

"Go ahead. Signor O'Lary is in the office."

They found Madame Firmino in Evelina's room. She was no longer in her dressing gown, but wearing a masculine outfit in iron-grey, with wide trousers falling over cork-soled shoes. She came up to De Vincenzi.

"All night I thought about what the police do when they come across two bodies and no definite clues that permit them to proceed with an arrest. You may be able to throw some light on this for me, Inspector, because on my own I couldn't think of an answer to the question."

She spoke ironically but looked feverish. Her apparent indifference masked a very serious worry, and her nerves couldn't have been the firmest or soundest, despite her sun cures.

"Madame Firmino, the police can do nothing but watch and wait. But who told you there weren't any clues in this building?"

"A clear, small fingerprint? Cigarette ash? So did the murderer sign their work?" She gave a fake laugh and turned on her heel so that she was facing Evelina's desk. "In the meantime,

Evelina is no more! And don't tell me she didn't take up much space!"

There was real emotion in her voice, but De Vincenzi felt the young woman was moved more on her own account than that of the poor spinster. It was easy to guess that Madame Firmino was afraid, and she'd probably barricaded the door to her own room the previous night. But of whom was she afraid? She leant against the desk, staring at De Vincenzi.

"What would you say, Inspector, if I packed my bags and returned to France? Would you try to stop me?"

"I believe so, Signorina—for the next few days anyway." He shook his head disconsolately. "I don't believe I can let you go."

"I thought as much!" She turned to look at Marta. "Cheer up, Marta! I'm thinking about a charming little design we could launch, a graceful cape in black silk, dotted all over with tiny silver skulls. It'd make a splash, and we could call it Number 13!"

"Dolores!" Marta exclaimed reprovingly. She must have been very upset to have used Dolores's real name. "Why not go and take the sun rather than standing here spouting foolishness?"

Madame Firmino shrugged and threw her cigarette on the floor. Just then, O'Lary appeared at the office door. He looked at the two women first, then at De Vincenzi.

"A good thing you're here, Inspector." His voice was shaky and his forehead pearled with sweat. "Cristiana phoned me just now from her room. She'd like me to go up there. She says she's found another orchid in her bathroom. Another orchid—and there wasn't one before."

"Oremus" was pale.

"I'll go up to Signora O'Brian. But I'm asking you, O'Lary: *don't phone to let her know I'm coming*. I forbid you."

He spoke so harshly that Prospero and the two women stiffened as if he'd lashed them.

4

On that rainy day the corridor was particularly dark and gloomy. The sphynx-like profiles of the white herms stood out against the frame of the single window near the service stairs, and the gleaming black-and-white floor added to the feeling of being in a hospital or museum, equally desolate places. De Vincenzi felt chilled to the bone. It wasn't just that the nightmare was starting up again, he quickly told himself, but that it was doing so at such a horrific pace.

He knocked once at Cristiana's door, and without waiting for a reply turned the handle and opened it. Cristiana stood in the middle of the room, her hands clasping crossed arms. Her head was lowered. Maybe she, too, was shivering, perhaps about to spring into action, whether to attack or defend herself. Her eyes were clear, her face wan. This time De Vincenzi immediately spotted that she really was deeply troubled. He hadn't seen her like this before, though he had noted her reaction when he'd shown her Evelina's body suddenly and without warning.

Cristiana started when she spotted De Vincenzi.

"It's you!"

"Pardon me, Signora. O'Lary told me you were troubled by the discovery of another orchid, and I thought it better for me to come to your assistance than for him to do so. If, that is, you need help."

Cristiana's nerves slowly unravelled, her tense muscles relaxed and a faint smile appeared on her face.

"As it happens, I don't think there will be any need for help. After those deaths yesterday, it's perfectly understandable that my nerves should be humming. That orchid gave me a fright at first—but it's only childish fear, with no justification. It's I who must ask your pardon, Inspector."

"Oh, but I wouldn't call your fear childish or unwarranted."

"Would you like to see it? It's an orchid, just like the others."

She opened the bathroom door and stood aside so he could go in first. There were two orchids on the dressing table, one in the glass vase De Vincenzi had seen it in the day before and the other on a pink cloth, as if it had fallen or was waiting for someone to reclaim it. The door to the "museum of horrors" was closed, and the latch still hanging askew.

"When did you notice that there were two flowers?"

"A few minutes ago when I came in here to take a bath and get dressed. I only just got out of bed. I had a frightful night, hardly slept a wink."

It had to be true. Cristiana was still in pyjamas and a pink bathrobe, with deep dark circles under her eyes that were surely the result of insomnia. Anyone coming in from the "museum of horrors" could have calmly put the second orchid on the dressing table, and Cristiana would never have heard it. The communicating door no longer presented any problems—such as the possibility of making noise. But why would someone do it, unless they were trying to warn and frighten Cristiana? For De Vincenzi, one thing was sure: none of his theories seemed to stand up in the light of this new and baffling event. He slowly returned to the bedroom with Cristiana behind him.

He was so perplexed he didn't know where to start with his questioning, though it had been his reason for coming to Corso del Littorio after his visit to via Catalani and Piazza della Scala, and his chat with Russell Sage.

Cristiana slumped into an armchair, the same one he'd found her in the day before. He looked at the bed. Of course the body wasn't there any more. The bed was unmade.

"Can you tell me something about orchids, Inspector?"

Her question was neither facetious nor bizarre. She really was longing for an answer.

"My dear Signora, I can tell you, based on my school memories and the encyclopedia I studied last night at home, that they are monocotyledons, extremely polymorphous due to a series of adaptations to environmental conditions and their means of pollination."

"Polymorphous?" Cristiana wrinkled her brow.

"Having many forms," said De Vincenzi with a smile. Then, after a silence, "Does all that help you to understand why someone would place an orchid by the two bodies, and a third in your bathroom?"

"No, it does not!" She sat pondering the situation with fear growing in her eyes.

"Did you know that Signorina Evelina was so worried for the past two months that she couldn't even spend time reading, which was her favourite activity?"

"Evelina? Why would she have been so worried? And why should I know anything about it?"

"Did you know that your husband has decided to settle in Milan?"

"Russell Sage is no longer my husband. I was granted a divorce before I left America. He must have heard about it on Alcatraz." Up to that point she had appeared depressed, lost. But due to her miraculous willpower, she remained wary and alert. "What else did you learn, Inspector?"

"Oh, not much more than that, Signora. Only that Valerio used to go to the dog races."

"Valerio? Not on your life! Last year I had to order him to go in order to get him to take one of my greyhounds to the San Siro Dog Track, and he still went only the one time. Fatima came last that evening, though she usually won."

"I suppose Fatima is your greyhound?"

"Was, Inspector. I had to get rid of her."

"Did she win many prizes?"

"A few."

So things were looking even more unsettling. The medallion he'd found in the "museum of horrors" might not have belonged to Valerio, while... But De Vincenzi didn't want to dig any deeper. He needed to gather a few more facts before beginning his offensive, which might even end in defeat. He stood up.

"Polymorphous... having many forms, right?" She was still thinking about the orchid. No matter who had killed Valerio and Evelina, one thing was certain: Cristiana was afraid of that third orchid. "Are you going?"

"Oh, I won't be able to leave this building so soon, Signora. But I ask your permission to visit the rooms I still haven't seen. Valerio's room, for example."

"I don't think it will reveal great or interesting things to you. Valerio was a bird of passage… He never settled down or built a nest. You'll find only a few articles of clothing and a huge mess."

But De Vincenzi found something else there.

5

The layout of the second floor was completely different from the first and third floors. When he reached the bottom of the service stairs, De Vincenzi found a short hallway with one door at the end and two on the sides. The door at the end was open and he could see a vast room with several tables, a rough wooden counter and a number of chairs. Although it was empty, it was obvious to De Vincenzi that it was the atelier. The dressmakers had left their work on the chairs or tables, and the usual large tailors' scissors could be seen on the counter along with irons, both coal and electric. Fabric pieces and offcuts were scattered more or less everywhere. On the right wall, two openings without doors led to two square rooms: one contained sewing machines, and the other a large table with cutting machines. And from behind a further closed door at the other end of the room came the muted sound of chattering and the intermittent clatter of plates and glasses. The dressmakers were eating. Once again De Vincenzi pictured poor Evelina, who'd told him she took her midday meal with the employees. Slowly he retraced his steps and tried the handle of one of the two doors in the corridor. It opened…

The room was empty. A bed with the familiar bedspread of grey damask, a chest of drawers, a wardrobe, a table and a few chairs. On the walls, several rotogravure pictures of cinema actresses and ballerinas snipped from Italian and foreign periodicals. On the table, a cheaply framed photo of a young girl whom De Vincenzi easily recognized as one of the models. This was Valerio's room.

He opened the wardrobe and saw quite a collection of suits. The young man must have spent all his money on clothes. Even the dresser drawers were full of fine underclothes, silk shirts, colourful pyjamas. He went back to the table. From a small bottle of perfume beside the photograph came the sharp and irritating scent of heliotrope. He hurried to put the cap on the bottle, but the scent lingered. He sat down and began slowly going through the papers lying around everywhere and inside the two drawers of the table. It was a slow process, since Valerio had saved letters from many women and bits of paper torn from illustrated newspapers and publicity flyers of all kinds; the drawers were full. De Vincenzi was rewarded for his patient sifting through all these papers with a precise idea of Valerio's character and intelligence. Even more enticing, however, was a cutting from an American paper which he now held in his hands. It had instantly aroused his keen interest.

He read the half-column from the news section carefully. It told of the disappearance of a gangster, Lester Gillis, who was renowned as one of Edward Moran's regular goons. The last time the man had been seen was in a bar on 18th Street. His disappearance wouldn't have aroused anyone's interest in the normal course of events, but some clothes and a few cards that pointed to his identity had been discovered on a deserted East River dock in Manhattan. The jacket had had a hole in it around the right shoulder, to all appearances produced by a bullet from a revolver. The shot must have come from close range, since the fabric appeared to have been burnt by the gunpowder. The paper's theory was inspired guesswork, but it seemed no one doubted that this had been a case of gangsters settling accounts. De Vincenzi pored over the cutting and on the reverse he found news from another city in the United States. That is, provincial news, as one of our journalists would say, and it provided him with the date of the paper: 12th January 1935.

How had Valerio come by the cutting? Clearly, he wouldn't have been able to snip it himself: in 1935 Valerio was hardly more than fifteen and living on the street in Naples, as Madame Firmino had told him, and he couldn't even have dreamt at that point that he would meet Cristiana O'Brian or Prospero O'Lary. No, this time it was a really miraculous coincidence. De Vincenzi folded the cutting and put it in his pocket before closing the drawers. He stood up, and as he turned he saw Verna Campbell stationed in the doorway. The woman was staring at him, a sarcastic smile flitting across her lips.

"There you are!"

"I saw the door open as I was coming out of my room…" and, turning slightly, she nodded towards the door opposite Valerio's.

"You lived very near the dead man, Signorina. How can you tell me you saw him only rarely?"

"I said he avoided being seen by me."

"Come in. Since you're here, we'll take up our discussion of yesterday."

"Your interrogation, you mean!" The smile disappeared from her face as she came in. Her eyes turned steely and her entire body stiffened. It appeared that the room awakened an irrepressible disgust.

"Why did Valerio avoid seeing you?"

"I'd appreciate it if you wouldn't question me on that point, Mr Detective. Valerio is dead and the relationship I had with him should be of no interest to you."

"Valerio was murdered, Signorina Campbell."

The girl shot him a fiery look. "Are you implying—"

"I'm not implying anything. But I'm looking for the man or woman who killed him."

"I might have done it, but I didn't. Someone else got there first. Someone who might have had more reason than I did for getting rid of that pest." Verna Campbell spoke with cruel resolution.

"Look, Miss Campbell, I'd like you to tell me exactly who this 'someone' is who might have had such a motive."

The girl's eyes shone with sarcasm. "Ah, is that all?"

"Of course that's all." He marvelled at his smooth tone. "Wouldn't you like to sit down? Our interview may take some time."

"I prefer to remain standing."

"As you wish. You see, Signorina Campbell, you've told me too much to be able to stop there."

"What did I tell you?"

"Hmm. Various things, which helped me to understand a number of others. In any case, assisting justice is a duty, and it won't do you any harm to carry out that duty. But we must continue. You've enlightened me regarding Valerio's character and morality, and in doing so revealed your hatred of him—your *current* hatred, which may have sprung from another feeling you no longer have for him, or at least believe you no longer have, for some reason of your own."

"Shut up!" She'd gone deathly pale and the order came from her lips with extraordinary vehemence. "Shut up! You have no right to root around in my heart." Her chest was heaving. De Vincenzi heard her grinding her teeth and, as he understood these symptoms, prepared himself for a hysterical attack. But through some extraordinary feat of will Verna succeeded in controlling herself.

"Where are you going with this, Mr Detective?"

"I'm trying to discover the name of the person who murdered Valerio."

"I don't know. But even if I did, I wouldn't tell you. I'm too grateful to whoever it is to betray them."

"Now think, Signorina Campbell. The person who strangled Valerio hasn't stopped at that. Evelina was strangled too. *And it's not over!* In some cases, a crime is nothing but the first link in a chain…"

"*Why should they kill again?*" Her voice was now shaky and her face had gone paler than ever.

"Because they've already killed, and because sometimes one must go on killing in order to try and save oneself. *Because this morning Cristiana found another orchid in her room.*"

Verna's eyes widened. "An orchid? What does that mean?"

De Vincenzi ignored the question. "Won't you tell me what you know, Signorina Campbell? Won't you tell me when you saw Valerio for the last time?" He paused, staring into her eyes so intently that she finally lowered her own. "How did you know, Signorina Campbell, that Valerio was dead and lying on Signora O'Brian's bed? The news of his death couldn't have reached you by the time I questioned you."

"Who told you I knew anything?"

"You yourself. You showed not the least surprise when I suddenly presented you with the body."

"Cristiana had told me that there was a police inspector in her room who wanted to speak to me. And she said: 'Valerio's had the great idea of getting himself killed and he's landed us all in it.'"

She looked away. What she'd said might have been true, but she was hiding something else—something other than the tumultuous storm of thoughts and feelings caused by discovering that Valerio was dead.

"Have you seen any orchids in this building, Signorina Campbell?"

Again, terror danced in her eyes.

"Orchids?"

"Did you know that the murderer leaves an orchid beside each body?"

"Yesterday," she murmured, almost whispering, "yesterday, in this room, there were two orchids in a vase. Valerio must have brought them."

"Where were they?"

"There, on that table." She looked at the table and remarked, "And now the vase is gone, too!"

6

It was four o'clock on that rainy Friday in March when events in the Cristiana O'Brian Fashion House began to spin towards their dizzying and dramatic conclusion.

But De Vincenzi had been expecting this for several hours. As soon as he'd learnt from Verna Campbell that Valerio had brought the orchids to Corso del Littorio, he made his escape and left the fashion house. He took the lift from the second floor to the reception area and rapidly fired off some orders to Cruni before leaving the building, under the confused and watchful eye of the quaking Federico.

Cruni's orders were to wait a few moments and then send away the officer and all the policemen stationed in the building. De Vincenzi had suddenly decided to lift surveillance and abandon the crime scene to the mercy of events and the will of the person who'd already killed two people and was surely contemplating killing at least one more.

Once in the street, De Vincenzi headed for a restaurant. He'd left Corso del Littorio so suddenly that no one would notice his absence, or at least not for some time. So he'd have a chance to eat before things started up again; he'd left the coast clear. That they would start up again, he had no doubt. Nothing that had happened up to that point could be anything other than preparation for the main event, the one for which Valerio's body had been taken to Cristiana O'Brian's bed and for which Evelina had been strangled.

He got to San Fedele at around two and found Sani waiting for him in his office.

"Anything new from Corso del Littorio?"

De Vincenzi shrugged—"Another orchid"—and went straight to his own room.

Sani understood his boss very well, and when he saw De Vincenzi lock the door behind him he said to himself that the latest orchid must in itself be an important development, one of those decisive factors that threw De Vincenzi into a particular state of turmoil and required him to seek solitude. It would lead to his taking decisive action and end with his explanation of the puzzle and the arrest of the guilty person. In fact, Sani immediately heard him pacing nervously across his room, another habit that revealed the intensity of his focus.

For his part, however, De Vincenzi wasn't even trying to find an explanation for the mystery this time. *He was sure there would be a new development, in itself illuminating, and he was waiting for it.* It was the anxiety of expectation that made him nervy, both with himself and others. Whoever had let the furies loose with the crimes in the Cristiana O'Brian Fashion House was unable to stop, wait or call things off. He'd have to act quickly, though, as indicated by the third, ominous orchid... He struggled to gain control of his nerves, forcing himself not to think of the ordeal. But it required too much effort, so he decided to reconstruct the events of the last twenty-four hours. He went over them methodically and meticulously, starting from the moment he'd stepped into the building on Corso del Littorio.

The principal figures appeared to be Cristiana, Prospero O'Lary, Madame Firmino, Clara and... Verna. It was she who stood out in his memory, troublingly and all the more painfully because of her fierce cynicism. Then there was little Rosetta, with her plait like a mouse's tail twisted round her head. Had the assistant really played no part in it? He'd bungled things by not questioning her. He'd surely have been able to get something out of her, since girls of her age are very curious and nosy…

One figure stood out from the others, like an obsession. There were no firm clues to set this person apart, yet he was basing all his theories on them, theories that had seen him practically flee from the fashion house, convinced that only in that way would he be able to return at the right moment. Naturally, he might be mistaken, and it was of course a serious risk he was taking—at the very least, he risked never being able to solve the mystery.

Three orchids: three bodies. At the moment there were only two bodies. Even though he believed his hunch was correct and would prove to be so, by removing himself from the scene he was setting himself up to stumble across another body before he could intervene.

He looked at his watch mechanically: it was three. At that very moment the telephone on his table rang. Instantly, he felt as if a great weight had been lifted. He approached the phone with the firm conviction that, for him, this was the beginning of the end, the final halloo of the hunt when it sights the fox.

A loud voice bloomed into the earpiece, making it vibrate. A voice both warm and instantly enveloping that came across as immediately likeable, even though it was mangling the Italian, twisting it with a foreign accent.

"Mr Detective De Vincenzi?"

"Yes. Go ahead, Signor Bolton."

"Aha! You're choosing the name you want, Mr Detective. So may I call myself John Bolton without being corrected? Thank you."

"Call yourself whatever you like, Signor Moran."

"Bolton! That's better, thank you."

"So?"

"I've been thinking, Signor Policeman."

"And?"

"I'd like to see you again. The fruit of my reflections may interest you. However, I wouldn't like to come to you…" The earpiece buzzed even more when the peerless John Bolton laughed. De Vincenzi had to hold the receiver away from his ear to preserve his hearing. When he put it back, Bolton had finished laughing. "It would be the first time I'd come spontaneously and willingly to a police station—and that would seem excessive, truly excessive."

"I've got it, Signor Bolton. You're worried that someone might see you?"

"A precaution, Mr Detective, a precaution. Well, what do you say to coming here to see me?"

"Now?"

"Oh yes, better now."

It wasn't the call De Vincenzi had been expecting. At least, the tenor of the communication didn't seem to be what he was waiting for. And yet he felt strangely calm and contented. The wheels had been set in motion, the gears were working. It wasn't because of his reflections that Bolton-Moran wanted to speak to him. It must have been some new thing urging him to reveal to De Vincenzi a detail he'd kept back at first. Some new thing, which the third orchid had foreshadowed that morning.

The telephone rang again. Corso del Littorio was calling: it was Madame Firmino.

"Inspector!" Her voice was broken, almost sobbing. "I found—I found a vase full of orchids. It was hidden. And don't laugh at me, Signor Inspector, but I'm beginning to be afraid."

"I understand, Signorina—and so well that I'll be there straight away." He hung up the receiver, put on his overcoat and hat. It had to be the beginning of the end.

Five minutes later he walked through the entrance to the fashion house.

7

It was Rosetta who opened the lift for him. Madame Firmino was in the corridor, apparently absorbed in studying some fabric samples by the light of one of the showroom doors. She acted surprised when she saw him.

"Already back?" She gave Rosetta a slap, shoving her towards the back of the room. "Go to the workroom."

The assistant trotted away and disappeared upstairs. Madame Firmino walked up to De Vincenzi.

"Don't say that I phoned, eh? The orchids are in the trunk room, the first on the left when you get out of the lift."

"How did you find them?"

"I looked for them. Nothing more natural than that they should have been hidden in a room no one ever enters."

"How many are there?"

"Lots. I didn't count them."

"Who do you think could have put them there?"

She looked at him suspiciously. "Are you joking? If only I knew."

She rolled her head, throwing it back as if in challenge. She did it to buck herself up, and quickly added, "If I knew, I wouldn't be so afraid!"

"Is there anything else?"

"Nothing other than that they've left me here almost all alone."

De Vincenzi studied her.

"You mean Cristiana is out?"

"Cristiana and 'Oremus'. Even Campbell, who must have gone with Cristiana."

"'Oremus'?" He wasn't smiling.

"That's what the models and dressmakers call him. It's Mr O'Lary."

"All three of them went out together?"

"No. Prospero stayed in the office with Marta and me. We thought Cristiana must have been in her room, but Marta went to see her and she wasn't there."

"What time was this?"

"It must have been two, maybe two-thirty. We looked for her everywhere but in vain."

"Are you sure she went out?"

"Well, where do you think she would have hidden? Her maid was missing as well, I told you. Of course they went out together."

"You're only guessing."

Madame Firmino shrugged.

"I'll take you to see the orchids now. Or maybe you'd like to speak to Marta?" She started for the door of the office.

"Wait a moment. What about Signor O'Lary?"

"Oh, he was worried about Cristiana's absence. When Marta and I went back to the office to tell him for certain that Cristiana must have gone out with Campbell, he was waiting for us in his overcoat and hat, ready to go out. And in fact he did go out right after he said, 'I think I know where she is. It's better if I go and get her.'"

"So where do you think she's gone?"

"I don't know, Inspector! You attribute to me an awareness of people and things that I genuinely don't have."

"You say this was at two-thirty?"

"About that."

He looked at his watch: it was three-twenty.

"Let me into the administrative offices. Then we'll go upstairs."

They went through Evelina's room. De Vincenzi paused for a moment in front of her desk. Evelina had been strangled between six and six-thirty, when clients were leaving the showrooms. Madame Firmino and Prospero O'Lary were in the office, where they were shortly joined by Cristiana after he'd sent her downstairs so he could be alone at the scene of the crime. He'd then discovered the body at around seven, while the two women and Prospero were in the office. *The person who'd strangled Evelina could only have been someone she knew well and trusted enough to let use her phone.* But he could now add another clue to the few he already had. Whoever it was must have come down from the third floor *in order to commit the crime,* since they'd brought an orchid with them, and had thus had to go and get one where they'd been hidden—in other words, the trunk room.

He turned to face Madame Firmino. "Try hard to remember, Signorina. Yesterday I left you in this room at six." He pointed to the door to the office. "You were in your dressing gown, chain-smoking."

"So?"

"When I came back later and told you that Evelina was dead, Cristiana and O'Lary were with you. Which one entered the room first?"

"Prospero. Cristiana came in a few minutes later—at least ten."

"So from then on, none of you left this room until I came in?"

The woman wrinkled her forehead.

"Wait… I remember Cristiana taking Prospero over to the window where they started talking seriously. I couldn't really be bothered about what they were up to. But yes, that's it. I don't want to tell you something that isn't so, but I seem to recall that at a certain point Prospero left, and Cristiana went to sit at her desk. But in any case 'Oremus' couldn't have been gone for more than a couple of minutes."

"Are you sure about this?"

"Sure? No. It's my impression that that's what happened, but I may very well be mistaken."

"Mistaken to the point of getting it wrong about whether it was Cristiana O'Brian who went out?"

"No, no! Cristiana went to her desk. I remember that perfectly."

De Vincenzi walked into the office. Marta was sitting at Cristiana's desk, and looked at De Vincenzi worriedly.

"What's happened now? Why are you back?"

"Nothing odd about my being back. What are you afraid of?"

Marta stood up and addressed Madame Firmino.

"Did you tell him that Cristiana has gone out?"

"Are you sure, actually certain she's gone out, Signorina Marta?"

Marta paled and replied in a high-pitched voice, "She's not in her room and I don't see where else she could be. If she was in the atelier we'd have seen her."

De Vincenzi went over to the desk. Nothing on its surface apart from the usual things. The drawers were locked. He remembered that Cristiana had been writing when he'd entered the room the day before, and she'd hurried to put away her papers in one of the drawers. He made for the central drawer, as if to open it, but he held back. He didn't have any right to open it, at least not yet.

"Let's go upstairs," he said. As they went through the office he remembered John Bolton. The American was waiting for him.

"Just a moment."

He went to the telephone and called the Albergo Palazzo. After a few minutes' wait, they told him that Mr Bolton had gone out, and no one in his suite was responding. De Vincenzi put down the receiver. That was strange. Bolton had phoned him to ask him to come to him *immediately*...

He suddenly felt nervous. The orchids were on the floor in a rough ceramic vase in the corner nearest the door, between the wall and a trunk. He counted them: five. The hiding place was just a figure of speech: anyone who came into the room would have seen them. Whoever had put them there must have been confident that the room wasn't often used.

He went back to the corridor where Marta and Madame Firmino stood waiting for him. He closed the door. Marta had been questioning Dolores and now knew about the flowers. She asked in amazement, "Are you leaving the orchids in there?"

"Of course, and I'm asking you to not to tell anyone—anyone—that we found them. No exceptions!"

Marta's eyes widened. Madame Firmino started.

"Inspector, you can't make me stay in this place!"

"Stay calm, Madame Firmino. Calm! Nothing has happened and nothing will happen... maybe. Let's take a look in these rooms."

But Rosetta came running from the direction of the service stairway. The young girl was pale and wringing her hands.

"There—there—on the stairs—"

She couldn't say anything else. She burst into sobs, covering her face with her hands.

8

Marta and Madame Firmino stood motionless, as if paralysed. De Vincenzi hesitated briefly, and had started dashing for the stairs when he heard the lift coming up at the other end of the corridor.

The doors opened suddenly to reveal Cristiana. As soon as she saw the huddle of people she started in their direction. De Vincenzi approached her.

"Where have you just come from?"

Cristiana had on a beaver fur with a matching beret. Her strange, pallid face was thrown into stark relief in the dimly lit corridor. She stared dumbfounded at De Vincenzi, the thin black lines of her eyebrows forming two question marks.

"From the street. I went out… You didn't tell me not to."

"You're right. But you should have told me."

Rosetta's sobs interrupted him. He turned round.

"Wait. Don't any of you move from here!" And he ran to the stairs. He only had to go down to the landing on the second floor before he found something, and that something was the body of John Bolton, alias Russell Sage, alias Edward Moran. The man had fallen dead just as he got to the landing, and half his body lay over its marble paving, half over the stairs themselves. The door to the second floor—the one that must have led to the kitchen and the workers' dining room—was closed.

De Vincenzi leant over the body. The man was lying face down. It could hardly have been otherwise, since just above his collar a black hole opened up his ruddy neck: a rivulet of blood streaked his right cheek and puddled on the floor. He'd been shot from behind and below. De Vincenzi felt his hand: still warm. As far as he could tell, he'd been shot recently, probably only a few minutes before.

He got up and went to open the only door on the landing. As he had suspected, it led to a narrow hallway one had to cross to get to the kitchen. Off the kitchen was a smallish room with long tables and benches neatly aligned along the walls. The tables were covered with white oilcloth. All the other doors were closed. De Vincenzi crossed the dining room to open the door on the other side. He saw the large atelier filled with busy dressmakers. One or two turned at the sound of the door opening and looked at him in surprise. Everything in order there. It actually seemed pointless to ask if they'd heard the sound of the shot.

He now knew exactly what he had to do, and each of his movements was swift and considered.

The door to Valerio's room was closed. Verna Campbell's was open, however, and he saw her inside tying a white apron over a black dress.

"Did you go out with Signora O'Brian?"

Verna glanced at her hat and coat still lying on the bed.

"I've just come back, in fact," she said.

"But were you with the *signora*?"

"Ask her."

"I will ask her. But answer me. How did you get here?"

She acted surprised and answered, "We came up in the lift. Cristiana went ahead of me."

"Was it only the two of you?"

"Who else would it have been?"

"Prospero O'Lary."

"No. We didn't see him."

"Don't leave your room. I'll need to speak to you again."

He turned on his heel and quickly re-entered the atelier. He spotted a dressmaker standing next to the table, measuring a piece of silk—its colours, flowers and arabesques gave it a sense of voluptuous heaviness—and addressed her.

"Has anyone come through here?"

The woman had a pasty face and her eyes were too pale. She was thin and miserable, but her blue-green eyes were alert. All the dressmakers were watching De Vincenzi with curiosity.

"Come through here? What do you mean?"

"Yes. Has someone come into this room with you? Have you seen anyone pass through the atelier?"

"No, no one."

Clara ran in from the cutting room. "What's wrong, Inspector? Who are you looking for?"

"How long have you been here, Signorina Clara?"

"For some time. This is my place, you realize—with the workers."

"Well, I'll repeat my question: have you seen anyone come into the atelier? I mean someone other than the workers. Signora O'Brian's maid, for example."

"No, Inspector. No one has been in here for at least an hour."

De Vincenzi glanced round. Astonished faces, spiteful faces, curious faces. Blonde hair, black, chestnut, red, in disarray. He nodded a goodbye to Clara.

"Don't let anyone leave this workroom. No one who's in here must leave for any reason." He went back through the kitchen to the landing. He passed the body and hurriedly descended the stairs. When he got to the foyer at the bottom, the service doorway was ajar. Anyone could have come and gone through it.

He went back upstairs to the first floor. He ran towards the offices, threw open the doors and flew through to administration. Prospero O'Lary was sitting at his desk consulting some papers. De Vincenzi gave no sign of surprise.

"Already back?"

The little man leapt to his feet.

"You're here, Inspector? What else has happened?"

"Nothing. Aren't the two bodies from yesterday enough for you, Signor O'Lary?" De Vincenzi's tone was facetious. He shot Prospero a friendly look.

"Oremus" put a hand to his head, then let it fall to smooth the lapels of his frock coat.

"For me? Oh! For me…"

"Where have you been, Signor O'Lary?"

"Why? Why are you asking where I've been?" He was trying—and failing—to maintain his composure.

"You must tell me. Signora Cristiana O'Brian went out too and everyone is worried about her absence."

Prospero's face lit up, and he immediately seemed more sure of himself. "In fact, I went out to look for Cristiana. Ask Marta and Madame Firmino. They'll tell you that…"

De Vincenzi slowly nodded.

"Leave Marta and Madame Firmino out of this. They've already told me. I don't doubt what you're telling me, Signor

O'Lary. I just want you to explain why Cristiana's sudden absence worried you so much that you ran out to find her."

"After everything that's happened her absence could only be strange, no?"

"Where did you go to look for her?"

He hesitated, then stated vigorously, "I'm asking you not to press this point, Inspector. The lady's private life does not concern you."

"Oh, you think not? Well, did you find her?"

"No. My guess was completely mistaken. Cristiana hadn't gone where I went to look for her."

"To the Albergo Palazzo? To her husband?"

The man was startled. "So how would I have known that Moran was at the Albergo Palazzo?"

"You didn't know, of course. The only one who knew was he—or she—who sent him the invitation and the plan of this building."

"The plan?"

De Vincenzi moved away from the desk. "It's an old story." He made for the door, and turned round.

"Where can Signora O'Brian have gone? You'll need to help us if we are to look for her."

"But has she really not returned?" He was genuinely surprised.

"You see, O'Lary, I actually think you need to start telling me at least some of the many things you're hiding! Valerio wasn't killed in Cristiana's bedroom. He was strangled in the 'museum of horrors', amongst the mannequins, and in the spot where he was killed I found a medallion from the San Siro Dog Track, which most likely belonged to Cristiana O'Brian."

"Oh!" "Oremus" raised his hands in a gesture of comic deprecation. "You can't imagine now that—"

"If you only knew the vast number of things I imagine, Signor O'Lary, you'd be surprised at how they can all remain calmly in my brain."

The little man went quiet and studied De Vincenzi more closely than ever. He seemed to be trying to decide something.

"You're right. We need to look for her. She may have got mixed up in something without meaning to. Cristiana has changed a lot recently. She's been doing things she's never done before. She started—yes, well, she's been using Valerio… The idea probably wasn't hers. I'm telling you, she's really changed, Inspector."

De Vincenzi smiled.

"I know all this by now, Signor O'Lary, and Evelina knew it too. *She was strangled because she knew it.*"

O'Lary opened his hands in despair.

"How awful!" He seemed disinclined to defend Cristiana. "What now, Inspector?"

"Nothing for now, Signor O'Lary. It's essential that I attend to the third body."

"What did you say?" He turned scarlet before suddenly blanching. "A third body?"

"Exactly! You didn't know there were three orchids? Just as there are three bodies…"

9

De Vincenzi turned his back on Prospero and headed for the telephone. "Oremus" fell into his seat, staring at De Vincenzi as if paralysed.

The orders given by De Vincenzi were brief. He asked Sani to hurry over with a few officers and the doctor. Cruni was to go immediately to the Albergo Palazzo and station himself in Bolton's suite. After a few rapid words, he hung up the receiver.

"So… it was Moran's turn this time?"

"Well who did you think it was, O'Lary? It couldn't be anyone else, *since he was the only one they wanted to kill.*"

Prospero's eyes gleamed oddly. Seated on a low armchair, he gripped his arms, as if preparing to spring up.

"And you think it was Cristiana who killed him? That's crazy, Inspector!"

"Who said that's what I thought?"

"Don't try to trick me! That's what you think, just as you think she's the one who killed Valerio. A single murderer committed these crimes. And if you doubted Cristiana after finding the medallion from the dog track beside the mannequins…"

De Vincenzi watched him attentively. Prospero stopped.

"Your theory is most interesting, O'Lary."

Prospero got to his feet.

"We've got to find Cristiana, Inspector. She's the only one who can prove her innocence."

“Where shall we look for her, O’Lary? At least you might tell me where you went.”

“Cristiana sometimes arranges to meet her friends at a pastry shop on via Santa Margherita. That’s where I went, and I stayed for over an hour but I didn’t see her.”

“Her friends, Signor O’Lary?”

Prospero avoided De Vincenzi’s gaze. “If you can call them that.”

“The friends in her address book, you mean?”

“Oremus” put a finger to his collar as if he were choking. “You know about that?”

“Oh, God! I’m bound to know *something.*” He turned his back. “We don’t need to look for Cristiana O’Brian. She may have returned.” He started for the door but stopped when he got to it. “Why don’t you come with me to see the body, Signor O’Lary? I prefer not to leave you alone.”

O’Lary joined him. When they got to the door to the corridor, De Vincenzi drew back to let O’Lary go before him. The little man walked quickly, but he stopped after a few steps.

“Where—where was he killed?”

“That’s right, you don’t know. Come with me.”

Prospero was silent for several moments in front of the body. Then, lowering his head, he whispered, “He survived all kinds of things in America only to get it over here.”

“Did you know him well?”

“Me? I hardly knew him at all. I’ve talked to you about him because everyone in America talked about him and because Cristiana confided in me on the *Rex*. But it’s the first time I’ve seen him.”

"Of course." De Vincenzi bent over to rummage in the dead man's pockets, and stood up again almost immediately. "Wasted effort. I don't believe we'll find anything interesting on him." The sound of steps came from the other end of the corridor. De Vincenzi went downstairs with O'Lary following behind. Sani was there with the other men.

"The body's on the stairs. Have it removed as soon as the doctor has examined it. The dressmakers will be leaving in a little bit and we can't humanly expect them to see this. The magistrate will understand. In any case, Sani, do let him know straight away. If he can come promptly, all the better." He put two officers on guard in the corridor and got into the lift. "Stay here," he said to O'Lary.

The women were in Cristiana's room. Rosetta was leaning against the wall near the door, no longer sobbing, though her eyes were still full of tears. The young woman had obviously let it be known that she'd seen the body because Cristiana, still in her hat and fur, looked terrified. Marta and Madame Firmino ran anxiously towards the inspector.

"Is it really Mr Bolton?" Marta asked. "Rosetta says she recognized him by his coat."

"Well, Rosetta wasn't mistaken."

"But why? Why would they kill an American no one knew? And why was he coming up the service stairs? Everything that's happened here since yesterday is insane!"

De Vincenzi shrugged. By this time he knew that insanity had nothing whatever to do with any of it. The murderer had calculated perfectly, knowing how to make the most of every opportunity with an astonishing readiness and facility.

"If I manage to expose them," he told himself, "I'll consider myself lucky. My having guessed who it is means nothing at this stage, since not only do I lack an ounce of proof, but to all appearances I'm mistaken."

He approached the assistant. "Where were you coming from when you saw him?"

Rosetta responded in a broken voice, "I was coming from the atelier. Madame—" and she pointed to Dolores "—had sent me away from the offices but I had to go back down to the first floor, because there wouldn't have been anyone on the door if any clients had come."

"Why did you come back up here instead of going to the atelier?"

"I heard Signorina Marta's voice."

That must have been just when he'd finished his inspection of the trunk room and Marta and Madame Firmino were standing at the top of the service stairs.

"Did you hear anything before you left the atelier? The sound of a shot?"

"No."

"Go back to the atelier and don't say a thing to anyone about what's happened." He took her to the corridor and sent her down in the lift. When he re-entered the room, Cristiana was sitting down.

"I'm sorry, Signora, but it's essential that you go down to the first floor. Madame Firmino and Marta will go with you."

Cristiana looked at him in surprise, but after a brief hesitation she began removing her fur beret and stood up. She threw her beret and fur on the bed and headed for the corridor. From the doorway she said ironically, "The body wasn't found on my bed this time, Inspector!"

"Sure enough. But perhaps it was only because of Rosetta that it was left on the stairs."

The woman flinched, and seemed to shudder convulsively. Her glowing, almond-shaped eyes looked enormous.

"Do you think… do you think they wanted to…"

De Vincenzi pressed her gently. "Oh, no one knows yet what they wanted. But don't think about that now. One fact is certain in any case: they won't kill anyone else and you won't find another orchid."

Cristiana said nothing. She moved robotically. Madame Firmino and Marta followed behind her and De Vincenzi. De Vincenzi pressed the call button when they got to the lift, and as they waited he asked, "Would you like to tell me where you were today?"

Cristiana revived, and murmured, "You won't believe me."

"That doesn't matter. Tell me anyway."

"I went to see my husband—the man who used to be my husband. I had Campbell come with me because I was afraid to see him by myself."

"Did you speak to him?"

"Yes."

"What time was it?"

"Before three. I'd left the hotel before three. We only said a few words to each other."

"Did you see him on his own?"

"Yes."

"In his suite?"

"In a sitting room full of flowers." She smiled sadly. "He loves flowers..."

The click of the lift was heard as it arrived at their floor.

"Well, Edward Moran *loved* flowers, but there weren't any orchids amongst the flowers you saw yesterday. I thank you, Signora."

Alone once more, De Vincenzi went into the trunk room. He took an orchid from the five that were left and returned with it to Cristiana's room.

10

He put the orchid in a glass filled with tap water from the sink, then opened the door and went into the "museum of horrors".

It was a ruse. He was preparing a trap. Maybe the suspect would fall for it, maybe not. In any case he had little choice, since he had few cards to play in order to confuse him and get him to betray himself. So he wasn't playing fair and square? Well, neither was the murderer.

Never before had he come up against a suspect with both the desire and the know-how to assemble so much damning evidence against an innocent person in order to get them convicted. And purely to save himself: such villainy enraged him. No, he had no scruples about preparing a trap for someone who, during the previous forty-eight hours, had done nothing but set traps and manipulate appearances.

Glass and flower in hand, he weaved through the mannequins. It was easy to find the spot where the overturned mannequin had provided evidence of a struggle. He set the glass on the floor and walked over to the door to the corridor. He remained in the room for only seconds, because from the moment he entered it he was suffused with the same strange uneasiness he'd sensed the first time he was surrounded by all those headless bodies.

He called down to Sani from the top of the stairs, and Sani came up with the doctor.

"I've finished, Inspector. There wasn't much to do, actually. The bullet entered his skull from the neck. In all probability, it damaged the spinal cord: death would have been instant. You see, Inspector—"

De Vincenzi interrupted him with a curt gesture. It wasn't the moment to listen to the good man's disquisition.

"Did you look in his pockets?" he asked Sani.

"Yes—nothing interesting. A full wallet and a passport in the name of John Bolton from Chicago. But here's what's interesting—look."

Sani opened his right fist. On his palm was a flower: *an orchid.*

De Vincenzi winced.

"Where did you find that?"

"In the victim's buttonhole."

Absurd. Edward Moran had put an orchid in his buttonhole? But there hadn't been any orchids in his room—he'd have had to procure one deliberately. Where? De Vincenzi took the flower, already crushed and flattened, and put it in his pocket.

"Good," he said. "Now go into that room"—he pointed to Cristiana's room—"and look everywhere. It doesn't matter if you make a mess."

"What are you hoping to find?"

"I don't know. Nothing specific. I'm asking you to do it but I don't have the slightest expectation that you'll discover anything of interest." He turned to the doctor. "I very much hope that this third body spells the end of your work here, Doctor."

The doctor didn't seem overwhelmingly troubled by his work. He shook his head.

"Oh, as far as I'm concerned…" he said. "Actually, Inspector, have you read my report on the first body, the young man's?"

"I haven't seen it yet. Strangled, right?"

"Exactly. But what you said following my first examination was right. Light pressure was sufficient to kill him. The victim was off his head—cocaine, morphine and alcohol. Whoever started pressing on Valerio's throat would have found him dead in his hands without even being aware of it."

It was all perfectly clear, and interesting—very interesting. De Vincenzi walked the doctor to the stairs with newfound gratitude.

"Thank you, Doctor. You've been very helpful to me. More than you can imagine." He shook his hand and went back to Cristiana's room.

Sani had emptied out the dresser drawers and was about to attack the wardrobe.

"Wait. I'll look in there. You take care of the rest."

The mess made by the person who'd hidden in the wardrobe had been tidied. The clothes were in place, the hangers all aligned. Nothing odd about that, since Cristiana must have been in there. He opened up a gap in the clothes and studied the back of the wardrobe. Nothing: he had to rule out the possibility of a passageway or hiding place. The shelf near the top was empty. He slid the hangers back, looking at the clothes mechanically, feeling the silk and other expensive fabrics.

All at once he noticed that one of the garments—a silk damask dress, soft and light—had a long tear at the neck. He took it off the hanger and examined it. It was ripped from neck to shoulder.

He hadn't expected to find such an illuminating clue. The doctor had said that Valerio was completely out of it… He stood silently pondering the revealing garment.

He turned at a loud exclamation from Sani.

"Look here!"

His deputy was getting up from the fireplace, a red lacquer box in his hands.

"It was there, hidden under the wood."

De Vincenzi smiled. The unhoped-for kept happening. He took the box and put it on the table. It was locked.

"Have you got a pocketknife?… Not working. Give me a shoehorn—that'll do."

He used the silver shoehorn to lift the lid, which was wooden and quite fragile. Inside the box was lined with red velvet; he saw a small bundle of letters of every shape and size. He sifted through them and established that they were all addressed to Cristiana O'Brian. After opening one, he didn't need to read the others: he learnt nothing from them that he hadn't already gleaned from his conversation with Commendatore N—. He closed the box and set it on the table.

"If I'd known what was in there, I wouldn't have broken the lid. It was an act of real vandalism, that."

Sani watched him.

"Love letters?"

"Call it love, if you want. You're finished, yes? Let's go downstairs and see if we can wind this up."

"Do you know who the murderer is?"

"Maybe. But knowing doesn't help at all! If I can't get them to trip up, they'll wriggle through my hands like an eel."

As they descended the stairs, they saw the body on the landing being watched over by two officers.

"Haven't they come from the mortuary yet?" asked Sani.

"Not yet, sir."

Bolton was now lying supine, and his round face bore his usual calm, smiling and charming demeanour. He looked as if he were sleeping. The bullet would definitely have struck him before he knew he'd been hit. De Vincenzi paused to look at him. His unruffled appearance revealed a lot to De Vincenzi. Bolton had been walking up the stairs, completely unaware that he'd been lured there. He must have been coming to a very promising meeting. *He'd phoned De Vincenzi to ask him to meet him right away, and as he spoke on the phone his voice had trembled with suppressed anxiety, almost quaking with fear.*

Bolton had phoned him at three, when Cristiana—if things were really as she had described—had already left the Albergo Palazzo. Not even an hour later, the man had climbed the stairs in the building on Corso del Littorio and had been shot and killed from behind.

What had happened in that short space of time to induce him to leave his hotel unexpectedly and throw himself into the dragon's den? He shook himself and turned to Sani.

"Would you mind running a quick errand for me? You won't have to go far, but you'll have to go quickly. I'll wait for you before beginning."

As they walked downstairs, he told Sani what he needed. Sani's face lit up.

"So you know, then?"

"Alas no, my friend! I'm not certain of anything. And what I do know is so hit-and-miss that if it turns out to be wrong, my job will be on the line for real this time."

11

De Vincenzi found Cristiana and the two other women sitting in the showroom. Prospero O'Lary was pacing in front of them. The little man's face was brighter than ever, his head shiny. He'd lost all the gloss of the pricey knick-knack, and despite his impeccable frock coat and glasses (which kept sliding down his nose), he appeared strangely different from before. One might have said that, stripped of its sheen, his humble nature was exposed for what it was, and he seemed rather common.

"You can't shut your eyes to the evidence!" he was saying, all the while pacing aimlessly. "You have to face it! When you're being accused of something serious, it's not the time to hide your mistakes, either from yourself or anyone else." He stopped in front of Cristiana and extended his hands in a dramatic gesture of entreaty. "You went to see Russell Sage and spoke to him. Right after that he came here and someone killed him. Who would believe that you weren't the one to lure him here so you could kill him? Of course I don't believe it, but the others? Why don't you admit that Valerio was blackmailing you? You didn't kill him either, I agree. But the fact is that that scoundrel left a lot to incriminate you. And Evelina? Everything will come out, I'm telling you—everything!"

His voice was low and breathy, but it was perfectly intelligible to De Vincenzi, who'd stopped in the doorway. Marta and Madame Firmino were listening too, completely astonished. Their eyes flitted between Prospero and Cristiana who, pale though she was, watched him, a faintly sarcastic smile on her tense face, now more inscrutable than ever.

At the sound of an officer's heavy steps coming from the lobby into the corridor, Prospero swivelled round and saw De Vincenzi. He immediately fell silent, biting his lip in a gesture of annoyance. Cristiana was still smiling. She too had seen De Vincenzi, and she said in a perfectly calm voice, "Now that you've heard O'Lary's closing speech, Inspector, there's nothing left to do but handcuff me."

Prospero erupted again. "Damn! Don't listen to her, Inspector. I know she's innocent. But I wanted to startle her so she'd wake up to reality."

"Of course," agreed De Vincenzi, and he turned to his officer. "What is it?"

"A woman is asking to speak to Cristiana O'Brian. They stopped her at the door but she's insisting. She says her name is Anna Bolton. When she saw the stretcher from the mortuary she started screaming and we really had to sweat to keep her from going after it."

"Send her up."

The man rushed off. The news that Anna was there had fortunately roused Cristiana from her torpor. She stood up and now waited, paler than ever and trembling with tension, her eyes fixed on the door.

Anna Sage was led in by the officer; he left at a nod from De Vincenzi. Edward Moran's sister was wearing the same black dress as before and a small hat with a veil. Her naturally white face was even more striking now. She was very controlled, but her green eyes flashed menacingly. De Vincenzi approached her in an effort to keep her in the corridor, but she moved quickly—her tread was so light, she seemed to have magical powers of levitation—and encountered him in sight of the open door to the showroom. It was exactly what De Vincenzi hadn't wanted and he stepped between her and the door. He might have asked for her to be sent up—a rash move inspired by anger and sorrow—hoping to glean some useful and decisive information. But he didn't want the inevitable conflict with Cristiana O'Brian to be too serious. Anna looked first at De Vincenzi, then over his shoulder at the other people in the room.

"My brother came here," she said in a strong, grating, cutting voice. *"He's been killed, hasn't he?"*

De Vincenzi had not been expecting such a direct attack. He paused.

"It's useless lying to me. Even if I hadn't seen the stretcher, I'd have been sure. When he left the hotel, he said, *'I'm going to see Ileana. If I'm not back within half an hour, alert the detective; I called him and he should be here shortly.'*" She stopped and stared at De Vincenzi. "Who are you?"

"The very police inspector your brother invited to see him."

"Right," Anna said, by way of conclusion. She fell silent. Her pallor had if anything increased, and she seemed ghostlike. To De Vincenzi she appeared to be swaying, and he made a move to support her. But she gestured for him to stay away.

"Did they tell you I screamed at the sight of the stretcher? I screamed, all right. But only because they tried to stop me from coming up. My place is here beside him." She shook her head vigorously. "To avenge him. You won't see tears in my eyes until I've had my revenge. How was he killed?"

"He was shot from behind. He died instantly, without suffering."

"Do you know who killed him?"

"No, not yet."

"I do!"

She stepped decisively past De Vincenzi and stood at the door of the showroom. She looked at each of the three women, one after the other, and raised her arm, pointing to Cristiana.

"It was her! His wife."

Cristiana flinched as if struck literally by the words; they sounded icy, lethal. Clearly gripped by terror, she shouted out in a broken voice: "It's not true!"

"She did it!" repeated Anna Sage, throwing another hateful look at her. She turned to address De Vincenzi. "Would you like the proof? I'll give it to you. You know she was his wife, don't you? Yes, maybe you do, but what you don't know are the reasons why she fled America. Not even my brother revealed them to you when you were with him today, because my brother, believe it or not, was a softie and loved that woman." She stopped and lifted the veil from her forehead, breathing harder as if to take in more air. In a different voice, trembling with a childish note of distress, she murmured, "Dead! She killed him! I didn't want him to see her again." Her outburst lasted only an instant. She immediately straightened up, cold and decisive. "My brother was arrested in a Miami hotel where he was staying with her. No one knew his real identity. No one suspected that Russell Sage was Edward Moran. However, one day the Feds went to the hotel and got him. She was the one who reported him. Betrayed him."

"It's not true!" Cristiana's shout was so piercing, so desperate that Marta and Dolores trembled.

"It is true. She's the only one who could have done it, and she did. Apart from the fact that she never loved my brother, she was forever anxious to be free of him so she could take control of the bonds and money. Edward hid them somewhere and told her. As soon as he was convicted, Cristiana disappeared. And when Edward got out of prison, the money and bonds were gone. That's the truth!"

Cristiana leant against the wall, staring at her sister-in-law. She seemed to have given up the fight and any further self-defence. Her staring eyes flashed with impotent desperation.

"Edward wanted to find her. After she'd run off to Paris, he found her here. He wasn't after the money. He would have forgiven her everything just to have her with him again. I told you: he was in love with her and thought he couldn't live without her. But she was afraid. She saw him as the avenger and killed him as soon as she could."

There was a silence. Anna Sage remained standing, motionless. Her eyes never left De Vincenzi's. She was waiting for him to exact punishment.

De Vincenzi wracked his brain. Things were finally where he wanted them, things were unravelling... It all hung on his not making the tiniest error, not uttering a word more than required—or failing to utter a necessary one. Everything was resting on him, from undoing the knot to revealing the truth—a truth that was natural, logical and unquestionably damning. There'd been another body, but it hadn't been humanly possible to prevent it. He now realized that he'd been deluded to think he'd be able to intervene in time. If he had, and in the only possible way—that is, by arresting the suspect—he'd have had to apologize and let him go. Edward Moran's murder explained everything, and it alone could provide De Vincenzi with the means of obtaining the evidence he needed to charge someone.

"Did you hear me? I'm accusing that woman of being my brother's killer!"

"I heard you, Signora."

He turned to look at Cristiana. Instinctively, Marta and Madame Firmino moved away from the woman who was in charge of the O'Brian Fashion House—and of them as well. Cristiana stood alone against the wall, unmoving. Her wide eyes never left Anna Sage. De Vincenzi stepped towards her, and Cristiana looked at him as if she were seeing him for the first time.

"Are you arresting me?" she asked. There was no trace of anger or fear in her voice.

De Vincenzi kept walking in her direction. He took a chair and pushed it towards Cristiana.

"Please, sit down. I can tell you whether I'll be arresting you within half an hour at the most."

Cristiana sat.

12

"Signora, your brother phoned me at three today to ask me to come and see him. He wanted to tell me something he had kept from me. Do you know what it was about?"

Anna Sage shook her head. "He just said that he'd remembered some detail about his life that might be of interest and have some connection to how he came to be in his wife's fashion house."

"He said it just like that?"

"More or less. Edward had just finished talking to—that woman. She'd come to see him and he was upset—I've told you he loved her—so upset he didn't know what he was saying. Several times he said the word 'orchid' and sneered."

De Vincenzi's eyes were gleaming. From the door of the showroom he looked at the people gathered in front of him. Anna Sage stood beside him and Cristiana was still sitting in a chair next to the wall.

"So he specifically wanted to discuss the orchid with me?"

"Oh, how can you think that? I'm telling you, he wasn't making sense."

"Signora, do you know what his wife had gone to tell him?"

"Yes."

"And?"

"Oh, that woman is a clever actress! She came to tell him to prepare to leave Milan with her. She'd decided to go with him as long as he took her far away, and immediately. A trap, of course, to get him back into this house."

"Wait!" De Vincenzi called the officer stationed in the lobby. "Go to the second floor and ask the maid, Verna Campbell, to come down here. Bring her here quickly." He turned back to Anna Sage. "And your brother came to this building? Why? And why, after a meeting like that, would he phone to ask me to go and see him?"

"It was after the meeting that he remembered the detail I mentioned. It came to him like a revelation. He jumped up and started going crazy, mentioning the orchid... Then he phoned you. I left him to go back to my room and a little later he came in to tell me that he'd be coming here. He advised me to tell you if he wasn't back in half an hour."

Verna Campbell came in from the corridor. She got as far as the door where De Vincenzi was standing and stopped.

"Signorina Campbell, did you go to the Albergo Palazzo with Signora O'Brian?"

Verna stiffened. "I told you to ask her!"

"Yes, you did. But I'm asking *you* to answer me, and I warn you that things are too serious for you to waste my time with your silence. Your mistress stands accused as a murderer. I'm telling you to make you aware of the responsibility you're under and the danger you yourself are facing."

Verna paled slightly but appeared unintimidated. She replied sarcastically, "In any case, Valerio wasn't worth the Signora's getting herself into trouble."

"Who told you it was she who killed Valerio?"

"Wasn't it? What do you want to know, then? She had reasons to kill him."

"How do you know that?"

She shrugged. "Look, ask me something specific and I'll answer you. Yes, I went to the Albergo Palazzo with my mistress. She was the one who wanted to go. So?"

Cristiana revived the moment Verna Campbell appeared. She stared at the girl, and it seemed to De Vincenzi that she was no longer indifferent.

"What did the lady do there?"

"She asked for Mr Bolton and spoke to him."

"Were you with them?"

"I stayed in the next room."

"Did you hear what they said?"

"I wasn't authorized to do so."

"But you did hear."

She smirked. "It was short. As he walked her to the door he said, 'We'll leave together tomorrow. Thank you, Ileana.'"

"That'll be all, Signorina Campbell. Go back to your room."

Verna hesitated. The brusque dismissal surprised her. She gave another of her sarcastic smiles and walked into the corridor. De Vincenzi watched her for several seconds before returning to the showroom.

"I'd say that things are now perfectly clear. Just a few brushstrokes, one or two touch-ups, and we'll have the complete picture."

Cristiana stood up. "So you believe, Inspector, that I was the one who killed Russell?"

"That's your sister-in-law's accusation, Signora."

"And I killed Evelina too?"

"We haven't yet spoken about Signorina Evelina."

"But she was murdered!"

"That's a fact, and a sad one. Very sad."

"Well it's also a fact that Valerio was murdered. Are you accusing me of that murder as well?"

"We need to take things in sequence, Signora O'Brian. To reconstruct the crimes and then reach our conclusion. Yes, everything seems to point to you. And since I want to convince you that our legal system doesn't act blindly, I'll clarify the situation before declaring you under arrest."

Prospero O'Lary interrupted. "But Inspector, you're making a grave mistake! What motive would Cristiana have—Signora Cristiana—for committing the crimes? And what about the weapon?" His voice rose even higher. "Have you found the weapon?"

De Vincenzi smiled.

"I haven't found it yet, Signor O'Lary, but are you really asking me what motive Signora O'Brian might have had for killing Valerio and Evelina? A short time ago you yourself—"

"But I—" the little man protested vigorously.

"I know. You told me so. You wanted to scare her into defending herself. That's fine. A noble intention, but pointless. Getting to grips with reality, as you say, in order to destroy incriminating evidence is not enough to protect someone. Let's mull over the facts, and you'll see that they reveal the motives. Please take a seat."

He pushed a few armchairs towards the people standing by the wall and repeated his invitation.

"Make yourselves comfortable."

Cristiana was the first to sit. She must have been worn out. Marta, Madame Firmino and O'Lary sat down after her. The last to take a seat—reluctantly—was Anna Sage, and she left an empty chair between her and her sister-in-law.

De Vincenzi briefly studied the four faces focused on him. "Now, let's begin."

13

"I'll be as brief as possible, and I won't make a single accusation that isn't based on solid evidence. Let's start with Valerio, the first to be murdered. As you responded to or even anticipated my questions, you yourselves shed light on him for me. A quick visit to his room served to complete my picture of the man. I can add that, whether you knew it or not, he was taking drugs and alcohol: the results of the autopsy left no doubt. Cristiana O'Brian found him in Naples when he was still young, and thought she could turn him into her devoted creature, someone ready to serve her. She herself defined him as 'an object', a loyal pet. And she used him."

He paused and addressed Cristiana directly. "Signora, I don't know if you did it because you had to, or because of some innate moral deficiency, but it's clear that from the time you opened this fashion house, you used it to squeeze money out of people with whom you came into contact, people who presented opportunities for blackmail. The proof is in all those letters and other documents you kept in a red lacquer box. It wasn't difficult for me to find it, even though you tried to hide it under burnt wood in the fireplace."

Cristiana muttered, "It was my revenge, the revenge I took against my fate. You wouldn't understand."

"I may well do, Signora. Perhaps your cynical way of profiting from others' vices and weaknesses comes out of rebellion, a cold determination to make everyone else do what you had to do—or believed you had to."

"My heart was poisoned! You have no idea."

De Vincenzi put up his hand.

"I'm not judging you here, Signora, I'm explaining. You used Valerio to carry out that sort of work, so he naturally knew all your secrets. At first he served you just as you wanted him to and in the way you felt one human being should serve another: blindly. But Valerio himself was unhinged, a person lacking morals or scruples, corrupted by passions and vices. Soon enough, he turned the same weapon you used against others against you: blackmail. And then *you* became his unwitting victim, and so you remained until you killed him—for some random reason which I don't understand, though there must have been one."

Cristiana looked up. "And would I have killed him in my room and left his body on my bed?"

"No, not in your room. Valerio was killed in the 'museum of horrors' amongst the mannequins. You quarrelled with him, or maybe had to explain something to him there... Or it could have been none of this, simply that he was in that room, there was a chance to get rid of him—and you took it."

The woman started to speak but she must have felt that it was no use defending herself. She shook her head and said nothing.

"There's proof for what I've said. The evidence, still in the 'museum of horrors', speaks for itself. And if that were not enough, next to an overturned mannequin I found a medallion belonging to you from the San Siro Dog Track. In your wardrobe, there's a dress—the one you most likely wore yesterday morning; it will be easy to find witnesses to swear that they saw you in it. It's torn at the shoulder and shows that you struggled with someone. The evidence in this crime is very clear, and all of it leads to you alone. The body's having been found in your bed isn't enough to demolish it, but it's not difficult to believe that you yourself took it there to muddle the picture."

Cristiana appeared resigned. There was nothing but a terrible, hopeless weariness in her eyes, and as she watched De Vincenzi a single plea could be read in them: Make it quick! Make it quick!

Madame Firmino and Marta sat listening to De Vincenzi's measured and terrible words. A feeling of horror had crept under their alarm and confusion, and they now felt paralysed with fear. Beside them, Prospero O'Lary seemed so depressed that he lacked the strength to intervene. Only Anna Sage, tragically immobile, continued staring at Cristiana. The coils of the accusation were tightening inexorably around her with the cold-heartedness of Nemesis.

"After you committed the first crime and thought you were free of the danger posed by Valerio, you suddenly discovered that you had to confront two other problems: Evelina and your husband. Evelina stumbled across one of your blackmail plots. I'm not about to tell you how I discovered it, but I assure you that I have proof. That poor woman, with her innocent, romantic spirit, thought she could come between you and your deal. She phoned one of your victims, made contact with him and promised to stop the blackmailing. The evening of the day she was strangled, she was supposed to meet up with Commendatore N—. But Evelina wanted to speak to you before her meeting, to tell you that she knew everything.

She was suffering from the shock of Valerio's murder, and thought you'd committed it. You were terrified of this new danger, and thought you could ward it off by removing the unhappy creature from this world for ever. You pretended to use the telephone behind her chair and then strangled her with her own necklace."

Cristiana groaned and Marta and Dolores let out a choked and horrified scream. "Oremus" shifted in his seat.

De Vincenzi hastened to continue. "Meanwhile, your husband showed up. His appearance just when Valerio's body lay on your bed was disconcerting for you. Not only did he appear as the material incarnation of your fate, the one you'd hoped to escape by coming to Europe, but he represented a settling of accounts you knew would be dangerous. When she accused you as she did, your sister-in-law revealed the reason you might have killed Edward Moran, whom you married as Russell Sage. You went to see him to suggest running off together, and you might have been sincere at that moment. But you feared that he might have known you were a murderer, and would thus have been able to keep you under his thumb for the rest of your life. You sent Verna Campbell to her room—after having asked her to accompany you earlier so as not to arouse suspicion—and then you phoned him, waited for him and shot him from behind."

It was as silent as the grave. The silence lasted for a few interminable seconds before Sani appeared at the first of the showroom doors. He took in the scene and then advanced towards the group. De Vincenzi turned to Sani, saw him nod in assent and then stood up.

“There you have it! Those are the facts against you, Signora.”

Cristiana stiffened. Her face was tense and she gripped the arms of the chair. “Are you arresting me, Inspector?” she repeated.

“For now, I’m inviting you to come upstairs with me to the room with the mannequins. I think it’s only fitting that I should present you with the evidence I’ve cited as incriminating.”

He turned to the rest of them. “You will of course follow me.”

14

The dramatic little procession was headed by De Vincenzi with Cristiana O'Brian at his side. Behind them Madame Firmino, Marta and Prospero O'Lary moved as a group. Anna Sage walked by herself, followed by Sani and the two officers who'd been guarding the entrance.

They took the service stairs, and when they got to the second-floor landing De Vincenzi stopped to let the others go ahead of him. He had an idea. As Sani caught up with him, he noticed the inspector's faintly ironic smile.

"It was actually here. He didn't meet anyone and he used the phone," Sani whispered to him.

De Vincenzi nodded in agreement. Cristiana, who'd got there first, stopped in the middle of the corridor. The others kept a marked distance.

"Signorina Marta, would you be so kind as to go in and open all the shutters? Even with the lights on, this room is unbearably gloomy." His tone was far from heavy: one might have said that, having solved the mystery, he was no longer interested in it other than as a pure formality.

Marta entered the "museum of horrors", leaving the door open behind her. Within a few minutes she came back and stood in the doorway.

"Come in," said De Vincenzi, and he ushered Cristiana in ahead of him. The others followed. Sani and the two officers stopped at the door. De Vincenzi walked straight over to where the mannequin lay. Behind him, the four women and the little man moved tentatively, afraid of being confronted with another body.

Cristiana suddenly looked terrified. Pointing in front of her, she called out in a strangled voice, "Another one! There's another orchid!"

O'Lary took her by the arm from behind. "What are you talking about!? You're crazy, Cristiana!" He immediately dropped her arm and hurried over to De Vincenzi.

"She's obsessed, Inspector. The fact that she sees orchids everywhere just goes to show how unbalanced she is. She's not guilty!"

De Vincenzi glared at him.

"Is that what you think, Signor O'Lary? *The trouble is, there really is an orchid, there, on the floor.*"

O'Lary raised his arms in a fury.

"But what are you saying? *It's impossible!*"

"Look!"

Prospero finally turned and saw the glass containing the orchid on the floor. The sight had an immediate effect on him, and his fiery red face turned blue. His arms fell back down and he stood staring at the flower, no longer able to speak or move, his eyes wide as if he were facing something monstrous and inexplicable.

De Vincenzi watched him for a few seconds and then shook him, slapping him on the shoulder.

"Come now, Prospero. That is the only orchid you didn't put where it was found, and it didn't get there by itself. It's a little trap I prepared for you so I could watch its effect on you when you came upon it unexpectedly."

The little man jumped.

"What are you saying? What is the meaning of this idiotic joke?"

"It means, Signor O'Lary, that I haven't swallowed the 'evidence' you prepared for me. How did you think I could reconstruct the three crimes as I did just now and attribute them to Cristiana O'Brian without noticing the holes in my theory? They were, after all, mistakes you wanted me to make. How could you fail to notice my deliberate avoidance of talking about the orchids? It was your brilliant idea to stack up the evidence against Cristiana O'Brian by attributing to her the obsession with the flowers her husband used to bring her whenever he returned home after an absence, even a brief one. As far as you were concerned, they would constitute proof of her cleverness in trying to implicate John Bolton in the crimes. But that would have backfired on Cristiana O'Brian herself, since in line with your plans for revenge, even John Bolton—or to be precise, Edward Moran—had to die. A really clever idea, and what a testimony to your cunning. However, it's precisely what's landed you in it now."

"But you're mad! Mad enough to be locked up! Why in the world would I have strangled Valerio and Evelina and then shot that Bolton man? I didn't even know him!"

"I'll tell you before long, Mr O'Lary."

He turned to the back of the room and called, "Sani!"

His deputy came running.

"Cuff him. It'll be safer that way, since it's possible he hasn't had time to get rid of the revolver he used to kill Moran."

With unexpected agility and strength, the little man delivered a violent blow to De Vincenzi's stomach, threw Marta to the floor to get her out of his way, and hurtled towards the bathroom door. But he didn't make it. The two officers on the door had got there just in time, and after a brief and intense struggle they pinned him down. It was an "Oremus" absolutely devoid of gloss, his frock coat in tatters, who descended the service stairs of the O'Brian Fashion House for the last time, handcuffed and with two policemen on each side. He was pushed into a taxi and taken to San Fedele. Meanwhile De Vincenzi, still somewhat pale from the stomach punch, ordered Sani to accompany Cristiana O'Brian and the other three women to his office.

"I'd like to wind it all up this evening. One cannot give a criminal like him any time to reflect if one is to trip him up. I'll be there soon, but first I'd like to have a final chat with Verna Campbell on my own."

It was eight that evening when De Vincenzi embarked upon the final scene of the horrific drama. Having begun in a fashion house, amongst the silks, lace and other fabrics, an environment of luxury and worldly frivolity, its denouement took place within the damp, whitewashed walls of a room in the police station, on the ground floor of a building that had once housed a convent.

Cristiana O'Brian, Marta, Madame Firmino, Anna Sage and Verna Campbell sat facing De Vincenzi's desk in his office as the head of the flying squad. Prospero O'Lary, no longer handcuffed, sat beside it, with Sergeant Cruni standing behind him. Sani sat on the other side of the desk. De Vincenzi spoke slowly, his eyes fixed on the sheets of white paper in front of him on which he was doodling invisible arabesques with the tip of a paperknife. On his desk, as well as the vase of orchids, were a pistol with holster and belt, a glass necklace, two envelopes addressed to Evelina Rossi and a red lacquer box. And finally, a crushed orchid that resembled a velvety, squashed spider.

"First I'll demolish the theory I myself put forward today in order to fool the real murderer into thinking I'd fallen into his trap. *Valerio*: the thing that immediately struck me when I saw his body was the fact that it was on Cristiana O'Brian's bed. It isn't possible for O'Brian to have killed him in her own room unless you consider this an unpremeditated crime committed on the spur of the moment. In that case, however, the body wouldn't have looked as calm, almost neat as it did. When I discovered later that Valerio had been killed in the 'museum of horrors' and was then taken through the bathroom, forcing open the connecting door, to O'Brian's bed, I told myself that this was a first-rate criminal, the kind in whom criminal deviation unfortunately assumes utterly ingenious shapes and forms. He'd have been able to conceive a plan which, *by constructing the appearance of guilt, would induce others to reject the idea.*

"Could Signora O'Brian have been that sort of criminal? Yes, she could, and both science and statistics tell us that it is much more common to find criminal brilliance in women than in men. But then there was the orchid, which had to have some meaning. What that might be I couldn't possibly imagine, and I admit that the real reason the murderer used that flower didn't occur to me until much later—that is, last night. When I got home, I consulted a book on American crime, actually written by the head of the FBI and full of interesting details on various famous gangsters, and Edward Moran's gang in particular. However, so that I can tell this story in the right order, I'll stop with the observation that that flower was capable of eliciting profound fear in Cristiana O'Brian. *That fear was real.* It wouldn't have been possible to fake it as it appeared in O'Brian. *Cristiana really was afraid of that flower.* Why?

"The explanation came to me today when she went to see her husband. The orchid was Edward Moran's favourite flower and he'd ordered all his gang members to use it as a sign. I learnt this from the book I just told you about, and Ileana Sage knew about it from the case heard in Rutland court. So when she found the orchid in her room next to Valerio's body—and because she'd already recognized Anna Sage in her showrooms—she didn't doubt for an instant that the crime was the work of her husband, who was using it to begin his revenge against her. And the killer had been counting on precisely this logical and inevitable reaction in order to get at Edward Moran—ensuring that suspicion fell on his wife. Isn't that so, Prospero O'Lary?"

The man sneered. "If you say so! But you'll have to demonstrate that I really wanted to strike down Edward Moran, when I didn't even know him."

De Vincenzi took from his pocket the newspaper cutting he'd found in Valerio's papers and set it down in front of O'Lary.

"Read that."

Prospero glanced at the cutting with a hideous grimace.

"So?"

De Vincenzi turned to Verna Campbell.

"Signorina Campbell, will you tell me who introduced you to Cristiana O'Brian, known then as Ileana Sage?"

Prospero broke in vehemently.

"I did! So?" He turned to Verna, his eyes gleaming demonically. "Careful what you say, Verna!"

The girl shrugged her shoulders.

"*You're done for,* Lester Gillis! And don't be angry with me. They'd have found out anyway."

Anna Sage stood up, astonished.

"Lester Gillis?" She peered at the little man. "Lester Gillis? But he's dead. My brother—" She swayed and had to reach out to the desk to steady herself.

"Yes, Signora Sage, your brother *believed* Lester Gillis was dead since he'd ordered his killing, and because Gillis's clothes and identification were found on a bench near the East River docks. Everyone believed it, as a matter of fact, and that's how Lester Gillis became Prospero O'Lary. But you see, like all such criminals, he couldn't definitively let go of his former personality, the one that earned him a place in your brother's gang."

"But he betrayed him!"

"Yes he did, and that's why Moran gave orders for him to be killed. However, the person settling scores threw what they presumed was his dead body into the river after they shot him in the right shoulder. *But Gillis was still alive*... so much so that when he got to the shore, he was able to make a run for it and disappear. You can't deny it, Lester Gillis, not only because we'll soon have your prints and photograph from the New

York police and the Kansas City penitentiary—where your long sentence must have been reduced—but also because you have only to expose your right shoulder to reveal your scar."

Prospero was still staring at Verna, his eyes burning with savage hatred.

"Bitch!"

"Leave it, Gillis. Verna Campbell took you in when you were injured and helped you stay hidden, allowing you to transform yourself into Prospero O'Lary. She hasn't betrayed you even now; instead, she tried to divert my suspicion from you by telling me she'd seen a vase of orchids in Valerio's room." He smiled. "It was actually that lie that led me to suspect a link between you, but I would have got there all the same. And more than likely, Edward Moran reached the same conclusion today at three o'clock, when he called for me to go and see him. The orchid was the clue. Your great mistake was to orchestrate such a clever and theatrical revenge against the man who'd tried to do you in, and to frighten Cristiana O'Brian with a sign from her past she'd hoped never to see again—a mistake so great that you're going to spend the rest of your life in jail." He paused. "And this one won't be like the one in Kansas City, where you can get out as soon as you've brought up more than your quota of coal."

15

It was nine-thirty when De Vincenzi wrapped it up.

"Let me recap, Lester Gillis. After you discovered Edward Moran hiding in Miami behind the name of Russell Sage, you found a way to make yourself indispensable to Ileana Sage. The Feds had just taken her husband away and it's my theory that it was you, rather than she—as Anna Moran believes—who put them on his trail. You advised Ileana to take the hidden loot and flee to Europe. When you got to Paris and found out that Edward Moran was looking for his wife, you were quite probably terrified at first. But you recovered soon enough, and made up your mind to get rid of him for ever, this man who not only inspired a hatred born of the desire for revenge, but who also posed a serious threat to you. You helped Ileana escape from Paris in time and establish herself in Milan under the name of Cristiana O'Brian, never letting your enemy out of your sight. Somehow—I'm not sure how, but probably by having him tailed by a private detective—you knew when he arrived in Milan. You then conceived your criminal plan, without worrying about the other victims and with the cold intention of allowing suspicion to fall on Ileana Sage. If you killed Moran and got rid of Ileana too, you would in fact also achieve your goal of getting all the money she'd stolen from Moran and then multiplied.

"You sent John Bolton an invitation from the O'Brian Fashion House, care of the Albergo Palazzo, along with a floor plan for the building on Corso del Littorio—all the directions he'd need in order to show up in the *signora*'s room, while Valerio's body was lying on her bed. From your point of view, Valerio's murder was a masterstroke. That irrepressible Don Giovanni had promised to marry Verna Campbell, just as he had so many others, and he got the newspaper cutting about you from her. He had the measure of your true personality, and having started down the slippery slope of blackmail, he didn't hesitate to try the same game with you after seeing how it had worked with Cristiana. A terribly dangerous game for him it was, and a fantastic chance for you to get rid of a troublesome blackmailer, ensuring in the process that suspicion would fall on the very person who had every reason to be rid of him herself!

"You killed him in the 'museum of horrors' and carried his body from there to Cristiana's bed. But you weren't willing to take any risks, and just in case the investigators should find the real crime scene, you left one of Cristiana's medallions from the dog track next to the overturned mannequin; it had been easy enough for you to come by it. I'll say it again: magnificent!"

Prospero O'Lary abandoned the farce of being the glossy and decorative "Oremus" and reverted to being Lester Gillis. He listened to De Vincenzi with a smirk.

"That's how you got things moving, and everything went according to your plan. Bolton actually did come up to see Cristiana and you hid in her wardrobe. It would have been very unwise to let him catch sight of you or observe you up close. You used your time and situation in the wardrobe to perfect the evidence against Cristiana: you tore the dress she'd been wearing that morning to make it look like she'd actually struggled with Valerio while strangling him. I'll admit that this little detail actually fooled me at first, when I found out about Valerio's physical condition. That is, I thought it really had been Cristiana O'Brian who'd accidentally killed him by unintentionally pressing too hard on his throat.

"But let's continue. The rest is pretty clear. Your second victim, Evelina, was forced on you by circumstance, and you made the best of it with some truly phenomenal quick thinking. At the moment, my reconstruction is only a process of deduction, but I'm sure it's not far from the truth. I'd sent Cristiana away. Upset by her husband's appearance, terrified by the orchid, confused by how Valerio had come to be killed in her bed and worried about the police intrusion, she goes down to the administrative offices. There she sees Evelina, who'd just been questioned by me. Aware of the deals her boss has been striking with some of her clients, and sure that it was Cristiana who murdered Valerio, she accuses her of the crime and threatens to tell me about all the blackmailing.

"Cristiana becomes even more terrified. She finds you in the director's office, pulls you into the window recess so that Madame Firmino won't hear, and tells you what Evelina said. You act decisively. You leave the office for a couple of minutes, strangle Evelina in the safest and easiest way, and go back to Cristiana—saying nothing about what you've done, of course. When I discover the body I'm already on the trail of Cristiana's blackmailing, and knowing what I do about Evelina's meddling at Commendatore N—'s, I can only attribute the second crime to her. I've said it before, Gillis: the planning and execution of your crime were top-notch, brilliant! What's left? Now everything is ready for you to kill Edward Moran, and it's certain that his death will also be attributed to Cristiana. You just have to find the right opportunity, and it presents itself soon enough. As soon as you learn that Cristiana has gone out in the early afternoon, you tell yourself: now's the moment. You go to the *pasticceria* on via Santa Margherita where Cristiana actually used to meet her friends and the clients she was blackmailing. You stay there long enough to be able to tell me you'd gone to wait for Cristiana and then you call Moran… I have no idea what you said to induce him to come to Corso del Littorio, and no doubt you'll never tell me."

Gillis's smirk grew more pronounced.

"Oh, no, I'm a good lad at heart, and if I can do someone a favour… Since I'm a goner, I may as well satisfy your curiosity. I told him a friend was waiting for him in Cristiana's room and that he should come to the via San Pietro all'Orto entrance and use the service stairs."

"And he believed you?!"

"Of course! I added that his friend would be wearing an orchid in his buttonhole, and that he should wear one too as a mark of identification, just like he did in America."

There's no one left in De Vincenzi's office apart from the inspector himself and Sani. Sani looks at De Vincenzi.

"Now this is over, too. Are you tired?"

De Vincenzi smiles at him in resignation.

"You can call this The Mystery of the Five Orchids."

"Five? No, three. One was my trick, the other a trick of fate. Edward Moran shouldn't have put that flower in his buttonhole. He really shouldn't have. He told me he'd changed his ways…"

Did you know?

In 1929, when the Italian publisher Mondadori launched their popular series of crime and thriller titles (clad in the yellow jackets that would later give their name to the wider *giallo* tradition of Italian books and films) there were no Italian authors on the list. Many thought that Italy was inherently infertile ground for the thriller genre, with one critic claiming that a detective novel set in such a sleepy Mediterranean country was an "absurd hypothesis". Augusto De Angelis strongly disagreed. He saw crime fiction as the natural product of his fraught and violent times: "The detective novel is the fruit – the red, bloodied fruit of our age."

The question had a political significance too – the Marxist Antonio Gramsci was fascinated by the phenomenon of crime fiction, and saw in its unifying popularity a potential catalyst for revolutionary change. Benito Mussolini and his Fascist regime were also interested in the genre, although their attitude towards it was confused – on the one hand they approved of the triumph of the forces of order over degeneracy and chaos that most thriller plots involved; on the other hand they were wary of representations of their Italian homeland as anything less than a harmonious idyll.

This is the background against which Augusto De Angelis's *The Murdered Banker* appeared in 1935, the first of 20 novels starring Inspector De Vincenzi to be published over the next eight years. This period saw the peak of the British Golden Age puzzle mystery tradition, and the rise of the American hardboiled genre. However, De Angelis created a style all his own, with a detective who is more complex than the British "thinking machine" typified by Sherlock Holmes, but more sensitive than the tough-guy American private eye.

His originality won De Angelis great popularity, and a reputation as the father of the Italian mystery novel. Unfortunately, it also attracted the attention of the Fascist authorities, who censored De Angelis's work. After writing a number of anti-Fascist articles, De Angelis was finally arrested in 1943. Although he was released three months later, he was soon beaten up by a Fascist thug and died from his injuries in 1944.

So, where do you go from here?

If you'd like another De Vincenzi mystery, get hold of a copy of *The Hotel of the Three Roses* in which our detective delves into a series of macabre murders in a seedy Milan boarding house.

Or if you'd prefer some northern grit, follow debt-collector Harry Kvist through the underworld of 1930s Stockholm as he tries desperately to clear his name in Martin Holmén's hard-hitting debut *Clinch*.

AVAILABLE AND COMING SOON FROM PUSHKIN VERTIGO